BABYSITTERS' SUMMER HOLIDAY

One of the counsellors on our bus stood up. "Okay, all girls out!" she called. There was a stampede. I was nearly trampled.

But as soon as I set foot on Camp Mohawk ground, I heard a familiar voice cry, "There she is! Hey, Stace! Stacey!"

It was Claudia Kishi, my best friend from Stoneybrook. With her were Kristy Thomas, Dawn Schafer, Jessi Ramsey, Mary Anne Spier, and Mallory Pike.

"Hi you lot!" I was *so* glad to see them. I ran to them and we began jumping up and down.

"Together again! The Babysitters Club is together again!" exclaimed Claudia.

The Babysitters are so excited! This summer they're going to Camp Mohawk, and so are some of the children they sit for. It will be just like babysitting – in the woods!

D0528064

BABYSITTERS' SUMMER HOLIDAY

Ann M. Martin

Hippo Books
Scholastic Children's Books
London

For Jean, Barry, and Bonkie

Scholastic Children's Books,
Scholastic Publications Ltd,
7-9 Pratt Street, London NW1 0AE, UK

Scholastic Inc.,
730 Broadway, New York, NY 10003, USA

Scholastic Canada Ltd,
123 Newkirk Road, Richmond Hill,
Ontario, Canada L4C 3G5

Ashton Scholastic Pty Ltd,
PO Box 579, Gosford, New South Wales,
Australia

Ashton Scholastic Ltd
Private Bag 1, Penrose, Auckland
New Zealand

First published in the USA by Scholastic Publications Inc., 1989
First published in the UK by Scholastic Publications Limited, 1991

ISBN 0 590 76628 7

Typeset in Plantin by AKM Associates (UK) Ltd, Southall, London
Printed by Cox & Wyman Ltd, Reading, Berks

10 9 8 7 6 5 4 3 2

Dear Stacey,

This is your last chance! Won't you please, please, please come to Camp Mohawk with us this summer? You can still sign up. We know because it took MaryAnne all this time to make up her mind about camp and she just signed up last week and the director said, "Oh, thank goodness, we need more CITs." (Really, she did say that.) But the deadline is coming up in two weeks.

So you've got time, if you hurry. Being CITs together would be so much fun, especially since now all the rest of the Babysitters Club (well, except for Shannon Kilbourne) is going to be at Camp Mohawk for two weeks. Even Logan is going. Won't the New York branch of the club please come? Think of the fun we'll have -- swimming, boating, hiking, meeting boy CITs.
Stacey, come on!
Love Kristy, Claudia, MaryAnne, LOGAN, Dawn, Jessi, and Mallory

Saturday

Dear Mum and Dad,

Well, here I am at Camp Mohawk. I have to admit it's very pretty, which is a relief. I really thought I'd miss skyscrapers and cars and especially department stores. But I don't-yet. The ride up here was awful since I didn't know any of the kids, and they mostly knew each other. When I got off the bus, though, what a reunion! The Babysitters Club was together again!

Mr. and Mrs. Edward McGill

14 West 81st Street, Apt. 12 E

New York, NY 10000

1st CHAPTER

Stacey

I'll never understand. How did this happen?

I, Stacey McGill, am a New York City girl. I love the feel of concrete under my feet. I love the sight of tall buildings. I especially love the sight of a really great department store, such as Bloomingdale's. Grass and trees and lakes? I can take them or leave them. Or I can visit Central Park. So how did I end up going to Camp Mohawk as a counsellor-in-training for two weeks? Well, it had to do with my friends in Connecticut. I lived in Stoneybrook, Connecticut, for a year, and just after I moved there, I joined a group called the Babysitters Club. The girls in the club became my friends, and we stayed friends after my parents and I moved back to New York.

One day I received a letter from my friends saying that they'd decided to go to Camp Mohawk as CITs for two weeks. They said being a CIT is better than being a camper or a counsellor because you get all the fun of being a camper, plus extra privileges, and all the privileges of being a counsellor, as well as extra fun. Then they said, wouldn't I like to a be a CIT at Camp Mohawk for two weeks, too?

I wrote back and said NO! I told them all the stuff about concrete and tall buildings and Bloomingdale's and Central Park. They wrote back and said, But Stacey, it's only for two weeks. I wrote back and said, So what? This went on for quite a while, until finally they convinced me to go. Anyway, how could I miss out on something the rest of the club was going to do? I couldn't. So I gave in.

I decided to do something special, though. I decided that if I was going to make this supreme effort—if I was going to give up two weeks of a perfectly good summer plus Bloomingdale's and my babysitting jobs in New York and all the rest—then I wanted some sort of a record of my adventure in the woods. I was going to keep a notebook about the two weeks at Camp Mohawk, and make all my friends write in it, too. When it was finished, it would be my book. We would all write in it, but the book would be mine. Of course, I would let the others read it any time they wanted.

So here is Chapter One. I get to write the first

chapter because the book is my idea and I'm bringing the notebook to camp with me from New York, and besides, none of the other club members knows about it yet. They will soon, though. Since the start of the Babysitters Club, Kristy has made the rest of us write up every single sitting job we ever went on. There's a huge fat notebook full of our experiences. Kristy could order us to do something like this because she's the club chairman, the boss. Now it is my turn to be the boss.

So. Here I am at Camp Mohawk.

At nine o'clock this morning, a crowd of campers, counsellors, and CITs gathered in front of a building on 34th Street near Park Avenue. It was the meeting place for anyone in Manhattan going to Camp Mohawk.

You should have been there. I will never forget that scene. It was a mass of parents, and of children aged six to twenty. (Well, the twenty-year-olds were the counsellors, and they weren't exactly children.) Half the people in the crowd were crying. That half was the parents. Also a few of the youngest children were crying. They were saying things like, "Is my teddy *really* going to be okay stuffed into my suitcase for three hours?" and "What if they make me eat *tur*nips at camp?"

The parents were saying things like, "Oh, my

7

baby. Going away for two whole weeks. You're growing up so fast. You'll probably come back taller than I am." (And hopefully cleverer, I thought.)

My own mother was saying, "Oh, my baby. Going away for two whole weeks. You're growing up so fast. What am I going to *do* while you're gone?"

She dabbed at her eyes with a soggy tissue.

"You could go to Bloomingdale's," I suggested.

My father laughed. "She could move *into* Bloomingdale's."

Then we all laughed.

While the laughing and crying were going on, the counsellors had been loading suitcases and sleeping bags and rucksacks into the luggage compartments under two buses parked at the kerb. Since most of us would be gone for only two weeks, not the whole summer, we didn't need to pack trunks and a load of other stuff. Only four children did. Anyway, it barely mattered what we packed in, because in everybody's suitcase were the same things: about three hundred pairs each of Camp Mohawk T-shirts, shorts, socks, sweaters, and nightshirts. (We were allowed to wear our own underwear and trainers, thank goodness.) And on every article of clothing, including the socks, was a teepee symbol. Now, I don't know a *lot* about Indian culture, but I know this much. The Mohawk Indians are part of the large

Iroquois nation. And the Iroquois Indians lived in longhouses, not teepees.

But what can you do? This was camp, not school.

By the time all that Camp Mohawk stuff had been loaded under the buses, the laughing and crying had just about stopped. Everyone was running out of things to say. But as soon as one of the counsellors shouted, "Okay, all aboard!" the talking and the goodbyes began again.

"Eat *all* your vegetables," one father said.

"Don't forget to feed my goldfish!" called out a little girl.

"Are you *sure* my teddy won't suffocate in the suitcase?" asked the worried-looking boy.

"Bloomingdale's won't be the same without you." That was Mum.

"Right. It'll have to close down." That was Dad.

This was getting embarrassing. So I hugged my parents and joined the queue of children streaming on to one of the buses. As I climbed the steps, I turned around to wave at Mum and Dad.

"Goodbye! Watch what you eat!" they called. And my mother added, "Have fun and be careful!"

It never, never, never, never, ever fails. Mum says, "Have fun and be careful," each time we say goodbye in New York. She's neurotic about it.

As nervous as I was about stepping on to a bus full of strangers, I did just that. While I was doing so I wondered, on an embarrassment scale of one to ten, just how bad "Watch what you eat" and "Have fun and be careful" were. I was about to rate them an eight when I heard another parent call out, "Remember to take your vitamins!" Well, there you go. That was a definite nine. I dropped my parents' rating to six and tried to decide where to sit. All the campers were sitting together, sharing seats, taking up whole rows. I looked for the CITs. They were doing the same thing, and I didn't see anyone sitting alone. So I started a new seat, hoping someone decent would join me.

Guess what? *No one* sat next to me. The bus wasn't full. Talk about embarrassing! I suppose most of these children had been to Camp Mohawk before, so they already knew each other. Why should they talk to someone they didn't know? It would have been nice, though. I mean, what was I supposed to do? I could pull out a book and start reading, but reading on a bus usually gives me a

10

headache. Besides, I'd look like a real bore. (Too bad, because I was in the middle of *The Catcher in the Rye*, which is wonderful.)

So I just sat there, stared out the window, and daydreamed.

The bus drove along Park Avenue for a while. Then we drove over a bridge and out of the city. That's an exciting thing to do, no matter how often you do it. I watched the scenery go by. I listened to the CITs in front of me. They were talking about makeup and clothes (not Camp Mohawk clothes) and Bloomingdale's. I wanted to join their conversation, but I didn't. I'm confident, but not that confident.

I remembered the first time the girls in the Babysitters Club phoned me to beg me to come to Camp Mohawk with them. Until then, they'd been writing letters saying, Please come, and I'd been writing back saying, No thanks, but the phone call made me start thinking. That night at dinner I brought the subject up with my parents. The first thing they said was, "But, Stacey, what about your diabetes?" (They say this whenever I want to do anything new.)

I replied, "What about it? I'll bring my injection kit with me. I've been away for two weeks before."

My parents were not convinced.

Diabetes is a disease which affects your blood sugar level. I have to give myself injections of something called insulin twice a day and stick to a strict diet, which means NO SUGAR, NO SWEETS. If I don't, I could get really ill.

Anyway, after quite a while, my friends convinced me that I should go to camp, and I convinced my parents that I should go to camp, diabetes and all. It was a tough battle, but for heavens' sake, what are they going to do when I want to go away to college? I'm already thirteen.

The bus rattled on and on . . . and on. We travelled along a motorway, then a country road, then a smaller, narrower country road, and then a dirt track. Finally we drove under a false wooden signpost that said CAMP MOHAWK. A picture of that teepee was at either end of the sign. A little way ahead of us I could see other buses. Children (well, girls) were pouring off them. (The boys would be driven around to the other side of Lake Dekanawida to their side of the camp.) Suitcases were being unloaded from the buses.

One of the counsellors on our bus stood up. "Okay, all girls out!" she called. There was a stampede. I was nearly trampled.

But as soon as I set foot on Camp Mohawk ground, I heard a familiar voice cry, "There she is! Hey, Stace! Stacey!"

It was Claudia Kishi, my best friend from Stoneybrook. With her were Kristy Thomas, Dawn Schafer, Jessi Ramsey, Mary Anne Spier, and Mallory Pike.

"Hi, you lot!" I was *so* glad to see them. I ran to them and we began jumping up and down. Then I tried to hug all of them at once, but it didn't work.

"Together again! The Babysitters Club is together again!" exclaimed Claudia.

We've been together a few times since I moved away from Connecticut, and each reunion is great.

The seven of us were laughing and talking and joking about our daft Camp Mohawk outfits, which look a little like P.E. kit, when a small figure came flying towards me and threw her arms around my waist. It was Charlotte Johanssen. She's from Stoneybrook, too. She's eight and was going to be a camper at Mohawk while my friends and I were there as CITs. I was her favourite babysitter when I lived in Connecticut. We miss each other a lot.

"Hiya, Char!" I said.

Charlotte hugged me and hugged me. When she finally pulled away, she left wet spots on my teepee shirt and I saw that her eyes were red from crying. Crying over our reunion? Crying from excitement over arriving at camp? I was about to ask her what was going on, when a voice came over a loudspeaker.

"Attention, campers and counsellors. Attention, campers and counsellors. Please assemble for cabin assignments."

Saturday

Dear Charlie, Sam, Andrew, and Emily,

Well, we got to Camp Mohawk safely. The bus journey was amazing a lot of interesting things happened. And your own brother was in on half of them. But somehow we reached the camp. One of the first people we saw was Stacey. What a reunion! Now we are in our cabins. We have unpacked. I've got the eight-year-olds. There's a counsellor, me, another CIT, and six campers in my cabin. Guess who two of the campers are -- Charlotte Johanssen and Becca Ramsey!

Love,
Your sister,
Kristy

Charlie and Sam Thomas
Andrew and Emily Brewer
1210 McLelland Road
Stoneybrook, CT 06800

2nd CHAPTER

Kristy

Well, the tables have turned, the shoe is on the other foot, and all that sort of thing. Stacey is making us write a book. Even Logan is writing entries for it. I suppose Stacey can make us do that. After all, I've made everyone write in the club notebook for ages now.

So here goes. . . . Well, our summer holiday all started because of Dawn. Dawn lives with her mother, and she and her mum get cable TV and have a video recorder. We get cable and have a video recorder, too, but usually we hire films to watch. Dawn tapes things she sees on TV. One film she taped was *The Parent Trap*. Another was *Meatballs*. They're both about camp, and Dawn watches *The Parent Trap* at least once a week, maybe because her parents are divorced and she would like to get them together again, just like the twins in the film do with their parents. Anyway, after the members of the Babysitters Club had seen *The Parent Trap* for, oh, the six hundred and fiftieth time, somebody (me, I think) said, "Wouldn't it be fun if we could go to camp? I've never been."

"Me neither," said Jessi Ramsey, Mary Anne Spier, and Mallory Pike.

"I went once when I was seven," said Claudia Kishi.

"I went for three summers in California," said Dawn. (Dawn grew up in California.)

Anyway, to make a long story very, very, very short, we found out about Camp Mohawk and we found out that we thirteen-year-olds (me, Claudia, Dawn, Mary Anne, Logan, and Stacey) could be CITs. Jessi and Mal would probably have to be ordinary campers, since they're eleven. Then our parents said we could go.

So that's how we ended up today getting a bus to Camp Mohawk, which is in New York State. Only we babysitters weren't the only Stoney-brookers going. Word about camp spread fast, and suddenly a lot of our younger brothers and sisters and their friends, and some of the children our club sits for, wanted to go to Camp Mohawk as campers. So my younger brother, David Michael, and my stepsister, Karen, were going. Jessi's little sister, Becca, was going. And most of Mallory's younger brothers and sisters were

17

going. She's got seven, and all but Claire, the very youngest (she's *too* young) got on the Camp Mohawk bus today. So did Nancy Dawes, a friend of Karen's; Charlotte Johanssen, Becca's best friend; Buddy Barrett and Matt Braddock, friends of the Pikes; Haley Braddock, Matt's older sister; and Jackie and Shea Rodowsky, children our club sits for. That made twenty-three of us—after Stacey *finally* agreed to go, and her parents *finally* gave her permission.

The bus ride to camp was pretty interesting. So was saying goodbye as we got on the bus in Stoneybrook. The counsellors, CITs, junior CITs, and campers gathered at the car-park at Stoneybrook High School, where my big brothers go. Parents, brothers, sisters, and relatives were there, too. It was chaotic!

I was there with Mum; my stepfather, Watson; Karen and David Michael (campers); my step-brother, Andrew; and my adopted sister, Emily. Sam and Charlie (my big brothers) refused to come. They said the experience was going to be one long, embarrassing goodbye scene, and they wanted to avoid it completely. They said they would rather tidy the house. (If Mum and Watson and Andrew and Emily actually got home to a tidy house, I would . . . I would . . . well, I'd do something weird, like eat my hat.)

"Where are you all going?" Andrew asked Karen and David Michael and me for about the twelfth time that morning. No wonder he didn't understand. We were going somewhere where we could play for two weeks.

"Couldn't you just go to the playground a lot?" Andrew wanted to know.

Watson tried to explain camp again. Maybe he should hire *The Parent Trap* for Andrew.

I looked around for Mary Anne and everyone, and stood with them in a tight, excited bunch. We talked a lot, nervously.

"I can't wait to see Stacey!" cried Claudia, but then she grew serious. "I'm worried about leaving Mimi, though." (Claudia's grandmother is not very well.)

"*I* can't wait to go boating!" said Dawn. (There's a famous boating scene in *The Parent Trap*.)

Not everyone was as excited as we were, though. Charlotte Johanssen was crying. She was standing with her parents, and tears were streaming down her face. "I don't want to go away!" she was wailing.

I was a little surprised when Charlotte had said she wanted to go to overnight camp. She is shy, has stage fright, doesn't have many friends, and sticks close to home. She's clever and sweet and kind and all those good things, but she's awfully attached to her home and parents. She's also attached to her best friend, Becca Ramsey, and her former best babysitter, Stacey. I think she wanted to be with Becca and Stacey for two weeks. Also, the Camp Mohawk brochure is glossy and has nice pictures of children going on nature walks and making lanyards in arts and crafts. Char loves things like that, so she got hooked on the idea of camp. But now that the moment had arrived. . . .

And it really had arrived. A school bus with the words CAMP MOHAWK and pictures of teepees on either side had just pulled into the car-park.

"It's here! It's here!" shouted David Michael. Unlike Charlotte, my brother was so excited about going away from home that he hadn't been able to sleep for two nights. I think Mum was a little hurt.

Several counsellors jumped off the bus and began loading our things into the compartment underneath. Around me I heard different kinds of comments—and shouts and laughter and tears.

"Ring us any time, darling," said Dr Johanssen, Charlotte's mother.

Charlotte's reply was a muffled sob.

"Behave yourself," Mum told David Michael.

"Behave yourself," Watson told Karen. Since she's only six, she'd be one of the youngest campers, but she can be awfully energetic.

"Dad, what if I don't like camp?" Vanessa Pike asked her father. Vanessa is a daydreamer, a poet, who's not terribly outgoing or athletic.

"If you really don't like it, we'll come and fetch

you," he replied, "but give it a fair try first, okay? At least a week and a half."

"Oh, *Dad*," said Vanessa, and giggled.

We children were starting to file on to the bus. I hugged Mum hard. I kissed Watson on the cheek. I tickled Andrew and Emily. Then I took Karen by the hand (she *is* only six), and stepped on to the bus.

All the younger children—Becca, Karen, the Braddocks, Charlotte, the others—sat together. So did we sitters. There were already a few other children from a nearby town on the bus and *they* were sitting in a group. We smiled at them. Then we began waving out of the windows to our mums and dads and step-parents and grandmas. I was sitting by the window and Mary Anne was next to me. She leaned across me to wave frantically to her father and nearly fell out.

The bus pulled out of the car-park. It drove down the street, through Stoneybrook, and on to the motorway. We were on our way!

A few interesting things happened on that bus ride. The first one was that Jackie Rodowsky, our totally accident-prone walking disaster, shouted, "Camp Mohawk, here we come!" and waved his special Camp Mohawk baseball cap out of the window. The wind caught it and blew it away. We all watched it bounce down the motorway.

"All heads, hands, and arms *must* stay in the bus!" announced a counsellor.

Not much later, Margo Pike, Mallory's second-to-youngest sister, got out of her seat, hurried up the aisle to Mallory, and said in a shaky voice, "I don't feel well." Margo gets airsick, carsick, sick on amusement park rides, etc. Well, now we could add bus-sick to the list.

We were about halfway to Camp Mohawk when my daft brother suddenly shouted, "Hey, let's sing 'Ninety-nine Green Bottles Hanging on the Wall.' " (He shouted this to the busload in general.)

David Michael is always starting this song and it drives me crazy. Only this time he started with, *"One million green bottles hanging on the wall . . ."*

I laughed. "Good joke, David Michael," I said.

But nobody else thought it was a joke. When the children finished that verse, they sang, "Nine hundred and ninety-nine thousand nine hundred and ninety-nine green bottles hanging on the wall, nine hundred and ninety-nine thousand nine hundred and ninety-nine green bottles hanging on the wall . . ."

They sang and sang and sang. By the time we reached Camp Mohawk, they were still in the nine hundred and ninety-nine thousands. But I didn't care. We were at camp! The girls on the bus got off. The boys were going to be driven around Lake Dekanawida to the other side of Camp Mohawk.

The counsellors were still unloading the girls' luggage when another bus drove into the car-park —and Stacey got off!

"Reunion!" I shouted, and my friends and I dashed to her.

I didn't know it, but someone was following us—Charlotte Johanssen. She had seemed okay on the bus, sitting with Becca, playing magnetic draughts, and occasionally joining in "One Million Green Bottles Hanging on the Wall". But now she was a mess.

She threw herself at Stacey, crying hard. I think she said, "Stacey, I want to go *home*!" but it was hard to tell because just then a voice came over a loudspeaker.

"Attention, campers and counsellors. Attention, campers and counsellors. Please assemble for cabin assignments."

The buses headed for the boys' side of camp. I waved goodbye to David Michael.

Camp Mohawk had officially begun.

Satruday

Dear Mimi,

Hi, Who are you? Fine, I hope. Im at camp it is so so fun. Well we havn't done to much so far but I can tell its going to be fun. I havn't ben away for a hole day yet but I miss you all ready. I realy realy hop your ok. so far we have are cabin asinments. Guess whos in my cabin, Vanesa Pike and Haley Bradock. Tonigt we have a group sing-song.

Love,
your Claudia

Mrs. L. Yamamoto

58 Bradford Court

Stonybrook, CT 06800

3rd
CHAPTER

Claudia

"Attention, campers and counsellors. Attention, campers and counsellors. Please assemble for cabin assignments."

We were in the middle of our Babysitters Club reunion, and Charlotte Johanssen was crying all over Stacey (while I wanted to hug her), and then that voice came over the loudspeaker.

"What are cabin assignments?" asked Charlotte as she pulled away from Stacey. She wiped her sleeve across her eyes and sniffled. Mary Anne handed her a tissue.

"That's when everyone finds out which cabin they'll be staying in while they're here," said Dawn knowingly. "We'll probably get into groups now—counsellors, campers, and CITs."

"And junior CITs," added Mallory.

"And junior CITs," Dawn repeated.

Mallory and Jessi had been made junior CITs. It's a long story.

"Oh, I hope I'm in Becca's cabin," said Charlotte anxiously.

That announcement practically caused a riot as everyone rushed for this big open area around a flagpole, where the head of the camp was going to get us organized. Since it looked as though the organizing might take a while, Stacey and I hung back from the rest of our friends for a few minutes.

I threw my arms around her. "It's so good to see you!" I exclaimed. "You look fabulous! What did you do to your hair?" I pulled away and held her at arm's length the way an aunt of mine always does to me.

"Body wave," Stacey replied. "I swore I wouldn't perm it again, and then it grew out and looked funny—sort of limp. And orange-ish instead of blonde. So I settled for a body wave. In fact, Mum *told* me to get a body wave."

"Your own *mother*?" Unheard of.

Stacey nodded.

"Well, I think you did the right thing."

"Thanks. How are you? How's Mimi?"

"I'm fine. Mimi's okay," I replied. "Not fantastic, but okay. It's funny. You know all the physiotherapy she's been getting since she had the stroke?"

"Yes," said Stacey. And we hurried a little to

start catching up with everyone.

"Well, it seems to be helping. We keep seeing improvement. But only in her body. Not in her mind. She's mixed up her sentences and forgotten words since the stroke, but now she's saying really odd things. For instance, she'll wander into my room and ask me what dress Patsy stole for the dance."

"Huh?"

"I know. What does that mean? Who's Patsy? What dance? And why *steal* a dress instead of buy one or borrow one? I don't get it."

We had joined the others and were standing at the edge of the big crowd of children. Stacey started to say something to me—to answer my questions, maybe—when we realized that the camp director was reading off lists of names and we'd better pay attention to her.

I knew she was the camp director because her picture was in the camp brochure. In a lot of places. Her husband is the director of the boys' side of the camp, across Lake Dekadonka or whatever it's called. Her name is Mrs Means.

Mrs Means. Funny.

And just as I was thinking that, I heard a girl next to me nudge her friend and say, "Old Meanie hasn't changed a bit."

Her friend giggled. "Yeah. Same as ever."

So *I* nudged Stacey and said, "Hey, Stace, they call Mrs Means 'Old Meanie'."

Stacey grinned.

We went back to listening to Old Meanie.

"In Meghan's cabin," she was saying, "the CITs are Sally Troner and Claudia Kishi. The campers are as follows: She rattled off a list of six campers, including Vanessa and Haley.

"Well," I said, "here goes. This is it." I looked at Stacey and at tearstained Charlotte. "I expect I'll see you later this afternoon or at supper or something."

"'Bye, Claud," said Stacey nervously.

I joined a group of girls that was gathering near Mrs Means. "Hi," I said to the tallest one. "Are you Meghan?"

"Yup," the girl answered cheerfully.

"Good. Then this is the right group. I'm Claudia Kishi."

"Oh, our other CIT. Terrific. I think we're all here."

Gathered around me were Meghan, Vanessa, Haley, four other girls about Vanessa's age, and an older girl whom I guessed was Sally, my co-CIT. She wore her brown hair in a French plait and reminded me a little of Stacey—sophisticated, but probably not snobby. I hoped we would be friends.

"Well," said Meghan, "let's introduce ourselves, even though we'll probably forget everyone's names right away."

We laughed but agreed to try it. "I'm Meghan,"

Meghan began, "and I'm your counsellor. We're in Cabin 9A, by the way, because you campers are nine years old, and we're one of the two nine-year-old groups. Isn't that an original way to name the cabins?"

More laughter. The introductions continued. The other four girls turned out to be Leeann, Brandy, Jayme, and Gail. I didn't remember their last names. I hoped I wouldn't need to.

"Okay, now comes the complicated part," said Meghan.

"Trying to repeat the names?" asked Sally.

Meghan smiled. (I definitely liked both Meghan and Sally.) "No," said Meghan. "Getting our luggage to Cabin 9A."

It really was a pain. First we had to find our bags, and of course everyone else was looking for theirs, too. The first time our group thought we'd got all our suitcases and rucksacks together, Jayme said, "Uh-oh. Where's my Garfield bag?"

We found the Garfield bag and started up along a path away from the crowd and into the woods. Then Vanessa said, "Um, Claudia? I don't think this is my suitcase."

We opened it. It wasn't.

So we had to go back. All of us.

At last, at long last we reached our cabin. We had walked a little way through the woods, but when I turned around to look behind me, I could still see the flagpole—the centre of the camp—

Old Meanie and a group of girls clustered around it.

"Here we are," announced Meghan. "Home disgusting home."

Vanessa Pike burst into giggles.

I took a good look at Cabin 9A. It was half of a bigger cabin. Guess what the other half of the bigger cabin was called? You've got it—9B. Another group of nine-year-olds, their counsellor, and their CITs would sleep in 9B.

Our cabin looked pretty much the way you'd imagine, especially if you've seen *The Parent Trap* and *Meatballs*. It and everything in it was wooden. The outside of the cabin was made from that rough wood—logs with the bark still on. A porch stretched across the front of 9A and 9B. Inside 9A were four pairs of bunk beds for the campers and CITs, and one single bed with a curtain that could be drawn around it. That was for Meghan.

Counsellors get a little privacy.

Vanessa and Haley immediately claimed a pair of bunks for themselves. Then Sally and I took a pair. CITs ought to stick together, we thought. Jayme and Leeann seemed to have been going to Camp Mohawk together for years, so they took the third pair, and Gail and Brandy were left with the fourth.

When the bunk beds had been claimed, everyone went quiet—for about five seconds. Then

Meghan suggested that we unpack. There were shelves along the walls and we were supposed to put our things on them and put our suitcases in the cabin's one cupboard.

"The room will stay neater that way," said Meghan.

So we unpacked. And we unrolled our sleeping bags on our bunks. While we did that, we began talking.

"Where do we, you know, where are the toilets?" asked Haley, looking around the cabin suspiciously.

"The washrooms are separate cabins," replied Jayme. "Group washrooms."

"Ugh!" said Haley.

The campers started laughing.

I climbed down from my place on the top bunk to see Sally, who was below. (I stepped on her hand on the way, but she was very good-natured about it.)

"Guess what," she said, when I told her I hadn't been to Camp Mohawk before, "there's a shop near the recreation hall where you can buy postcards and toothpaste and sweets and things." (Junk food—yum!) "*And* we CITs have dances and things with the boy CITs."

Really?! Camp Mohawk was looking better every second!

Saturday

Dear Mama and Daddy,

Here I am at Camp Mohawk. We got here safely and Becca is just fine, so don't worry about her. Charlotte is pretty homesick already, but she knows an awful lot of people here, so I think she'll be okay. Becca and Kristy will take care of her. (They're all in the same cabin.) Guess what — Mallory and I are in the same cabin, too! It's really half of a bigger cabin, and Dawn is a CIT in the other half. Our cabin is 11B. Hers is 11A.

I miss you, I miss you, I love you, I love you. X X X X X O O O O O

WBS, Jessi

(WBS means Write Back Soon)

Mr. and Mrs. Alex Ramsey
612 Fawcett Avenue
Stoneybrook , CT 06800

4th CHAPTER

Oh, gosh! My first time at camp. I'm not really nervous. . . . No, that isn't true. I am nervous. But I'm nervous about something most of the other children here don't even have to think about. I'm nervous because I'm one of the very few black children at Camp Mohawk. My sister Becca's here, of course, and I've seen two or three other black campers. But nearly everyone is white.

I suppose I should be used to that by now. I'm one of the few blacks in Stoneybrook Middle School—in Stoneybrook itself—and I'm one of the few black dancers at my ballet school. Still, I feel uncomfortable. I always wonder if I'll fit in. Thank goodness for Mallory. Having my best friend here really makes a difference.

Mal and I are junior CITs, by the way. We're the only junior CITs at the whole camp. We wanted to be CITs so badly that when our parents helped us fill in our camp applications, we added a whole paragraph after the place where it said "Comments". We each wrote: "I am a babysitter. I belong to a group called the Babysitters Club. We take care of children of all ages, sometimes even babies (but not too often). I have lots of experience with children. I would very, very, very, very, very much like to be a CIT. Could you please take this into consideration?"

Mrs Means wrote back and said that she wished she could let us be CITs, but that the rule is a CIT must be at least thirteen years old. Then she said maybe we could be junior CITs and help out with the younger campers, like in arts and crafts or on some special project.

Mal and I felt pretty special. That arrangement was good enough for us.

These are the other people in Cabin 11B: Autumn, our counsellor; Gwen and Corinne, our CITs; and Mandi, Maureen, Mary Oppenheimer and Mary Travis, the other campers.

WAHH! Every camper except me has a name beginning with Ma-, and two of them are named Mary. I really stick out. And I was really positive I wouldn't remember anyone's name except Mallory's.

When we girls from 11B reached our cabin, we stepped inside and immediately made mad dashes to claim our bunk beds. Well, Mal and I made a mad dash. We wanted to be sure to share a pair of bunks. But the other campers hung back, staring at us. Then they sauntered around and chose bunks as if they couldn't care less who they shared with.

Mal and I felt like great big babies. We knew we'd done something wrong. We just weren't sure what.

When all the sauntering around was over, Corinne and Gwen, the CITs, were sharing one pair, Mandi and Maureen were sharing another, and the two Marys took the fourth. Autumn got a private bed to herself, I suppose because she's the counsellor.

Autumn told us to unpack and showed us where to put our suitcases.

Mal and I unpacked slowly. We kept asking each other where to put things (as if there were much choice. Each of us has exactly three shelves along the wall by our bunks.)

Even so, every two seconds, Mal would lean down to me from the top bed and say, "I'm putting my toothpaste and things on the bottom shelf on the left." Or I'd stick my head up to her and say, "I'm putting my sixteen thousand pairs of shorts along the middle shelf."

Mal giggled when I said that. A few minutes later, she leaned over again and said, "Come on up to the top bunk, Jessi."

"Why?" I asked. "I mean, the bed looks as

39

though it'll fall apart if I climb up there with you." I stood uncertainly below her.

I heard little sniggers coming from Mandi, Maureen, and the Marys.

I decided the little sniggers meant that the beds were safer than they looked, that I should know that, that I could easily crawl up there with Mal, and that I was stupid for thinking anything else.

So I did crawl up. And nothing happened except that the other girls stared at us.

Mallory did her best to ignore them. "I made something for us," she said.

"You did?" I replied. "What?" Mal likes to write and draw, but doesn't often make things, so I was curious.

"Yup." Mallory reached into her almost-empty suitcase and pulled out two small bands of cloth. They were white. On each one, she'd painted a teepee and written JUNIOR CIT. "They're armbands," she told me. "We're the only junior CITs here, and I thought everyone should know it."

I wasn't so sure.

"Go on," said Mal. "Put yours on." She slid hers on and left it just below the sleeve of her Camp Mohawk T-shirt.

I hesitated. I glanced down at the M faces that were pretending to be looking at other things, but were actually watching us. I didn't want to put the armband on and be any more different from

40

the other campers than I already was. But I did put it on—for Mal. For Mal and me.

Mal is my best friend.

As soon as I'd put the band on, though, I whispered to Mallory, "Finish putting your things away and then we'd better join the others. I think that would be a good idea . . . considering."

Mal took a look at the other girls, then nodded. I knew she'd understood what I'd meant. So as soon as she'd finished, we slid off her bunk and carried our suitcases and rucksacks to the cupboard. We had just put them away and were trying to work out some way to join the other girls, when Mrs Means walked into our cabin.

Everyone became silent, even Autumn who'd been talking to the counsellor in 11A. It was as if we were in school and the head had just walked into our classroom.

"Old Meanie," I heard Mary whisper to Mary.

"They call Mrs Means 'Old Meanie'," I said to Mal under my breath.

Old Meanie spoke briefly to Autumn. Then she left. A sigh of relief ran through the cabin.

"Jessica and Mallory?" said Autumn.

The girls sniggered again. "Ooh, you must be in *trouble*," said Mary Travis, dragging the word out.

"Yeah, for wearing something that isn't part of the camp uniform," added Maureen.

"How could she have known about the armbands so fast?" asked Mal.

I nudged her. "They're *teasing* you."

"Oh."

Autumn stepped towards us, a smile on her face. "Junior CITs," she said. "I like that. You're the first we've had here."

"What *are* junior CITs?" asked Mandi.

Autumn tried to explain. Then she said to me, "Jessi, we've heard you're quite a dancer. Mrs Means would like you and Mal to teach one of the cabins of eight-year-olds a dance routine that they can perform in the show on Parents' Day two weeks from now. That will be your special project. It'll be a big help to us."

"Wow!" I exclaimed. "Mal, that'll be great. It'll be so much fun!"

The expression on Mal's face changed from uncertain to pleased. "You think we can really do that?" she asked. Then she added, "Of course we can. We can do anything together."

Autumn, Gwen, and Corinne wandered outside, away from us campers, which I suppose gave Mary Oppenheimer the courage to say, "Yeah, you two are like the Bobbsey Twins, the way you stick together."

"The Bobbsey Twins!" cried Mandi. "They don't look like *any* kind of twins, if you know what I mean."

I certainly did.

"I'll have you know that both sets of Bobbsey Twins were one boy and one girl," said Mal haughtily. "Bert and Nan, and Freddie and Flossie. How much can a boy and a girl look alike? We look more alike than they do." Mal crossed her arms and faced the other girls.

But the other girls looked pretty smug. "You still read the Bobbsey Twins books?" asked Mandi incredulously.

I stepped forward. I didn't want Mal to have to do all the defending. "Of course she does. We both do," I lied. (We've outgrown the Bobbsey Twins and are on to Nancy Drew—when we read mysteries, which isn't often. Mostly we read horse stories.)

The M girls laughed. "The Bobbsey Twins," said Mary Travis, shaking her head.

I looked helplessly at Mal. I was determined to sort out this problem. I just wasn't sure how to do it.

At least we had dance rehearsals to look forward to.

Saturday

Hi, Dad! Hi, Tigger!

How are you two? Camp is fine. I think. I have met all my cabin-mates and my counsellor and the other CIT. I just can't believe all the things to do here. We can learn to canoe or to row a boat. And we can work on arts and crafts and take nature walks and lots more.

In my cabin are a counsellor, another CIT (named Randi), and six campers, including Margo Pike and Nancy Dawes (Karen Brewer's friend).

More later,
Mary Anne

Mr. Richard Spier

59 Bradford Court

Stoneybrook, CT

06800

5th
CHAPTER

Mary Anne

Dad doesn't know it, but today I wrote him what was probably the least informative postcard he'd ever receive. It was certainly the least informative one I'd ever written. Suddenly I didn't know why I'd wanted to come to camp so badly. Maybe it was because it had looked like such fun in the films—lying around on cushy beds, daydreaming about film stars or boys, making lovely things in arts and crafts, finding new friends to tell secrets to. But mostly what I heard about here was sport. That was what the girls, even the little ones, in my cabin talked about. And the other CITs were really sophisticated. I got the idea that spending a lot of time in the arts and crafts cabin would *not* be sophisticated.

Randi, my co-CIT, reminds me so much of Claudia (only in looks) that it's weird. She has

47

long, long dark hair, dark eyes, and extremely fashionable accessories. There's nothing she can do about wearing the camp outfit—she has to wear it like the rest of us—but she accessorizes it beautifully. On this first day, she wore parrot earrings (Claud has a pair of those), a string plait on one arm, a wristful of bracelets on the other arm, and even an ankle bracelet over one teepee sock. The bracelet spells out her name. In her hair was a hairband with a neon green bow attached to the side. It clashed with the green words CAMP MOHAWK on her T-shirt, but who cared?

Then there are the CITs in 7B, next door. They came over straight away to meet Randi and me, and *they're* sophisticated, too. Their names are Faye and Julie. They don't look much like Stacey, but they act a bit like her (except not as nice). They're just so sophisticated and totally sure of themselves. Maybe they came on the New York bus.

"Hi," said one as they sauntered into 7A. "We're the CITs next door. I'm Faye, and this is Julie." Old film-star names, I thought. Faye Dunaway, Julie Harris . . . .

"Hi," replied Randi, as coolly as ever. She left her unpacking and walked over to the other girls. "I'm Randi, and this," she went on, pointing to me, "is . . . is . . . . What's your name again?"

"Mary Anne," I replied, blushing. "Mary Anne Spier." I slid awkwardly off the top bed of

48

the bunk Randi and I were sharing, and joined the other CITs.

"Have you been here before?" Julie asked me. "I don't remember seeing you."

"No. This is my first time. I've never been to camp at all."

"What did you do? See the film *Meatballs* or something and think camp would be a lot of fun?" said Faye. She laughed loudly, as if this were how all poor, unsuspecting, new CITs found their way to Camp Mohawk.

I absolutely hate meeting new people.

I paused, pretending I'd heard Faye's joke a billion times already. I smiled at her. I even managed a little laugh. Then, "No," I replied. "My boyfriend's here for these two weeks. On the other side of the lake. I just wanted to be near him."

Randi, Julie and Faye managed a three-way glance, which isn't easy. I knew exactly what they were thinking: She's got a boyfriend? *She* has? She looks like a baby. (Can I help it if I'm short?) And there is *nothing* special about her. (*I* hadn't thought about accessorizing at camp. I'd brought along everything on the "What to Pack" list. The list had not included parrot earrings or bracelets.)

"You—you, um, have a boyfriend?" said Julie.

Faye giggled, but tried to cover it up by coughing.

"Of course," I replied. I tossed my hair over my shoulders.

"What's his name?" asked Randi.

"Logan. Logan Bruno. He's from Kentucky. He has an incredible southern accent. You should hear it."

"Faye! Faye!" one of the campers in my cabin suddenly cried. "Faye, that girl" (she pointed to Margo) "took my hairbrush."

"I did not!" Margo replied instantly. "It just looks like hers. But it's mine. If she weren't so stupid—"

"Fa-*aye*! Now she's calling me stupid!" exclaimed the girl.

"Margo," I said, "don't call her stupid. Do you know where her hairbrush is?"

"Probably in her silly rucksack. I bet she hasn't unpacked it yet."

"Could you check your rucksack?" I asked the girl. All the while, I was wondering—how did this child know Faye, a CIT in the other cabin? And why did she ask Faye for help instead of Randi or me or our counsellor?

"My sister," Faye spoke up, "should not have to check her rucksack. If she says that girl—"

"My name is Margo Pike," Margo interrupted.

"—stole her brush, then she stole it."

"You're sisters?" I said, glancing from Faye to the other girl.

"Yes, and *my* name is Tara," said the little sister, looking pointedly at Margo.

Tara the Terror, I thought.

Margo stuck her tongue out at Tara.

Tara stuck her tongue out at Margo.

"I," Tara went on, not even approaching her rucksack, "bet you have never been to camp before. But *I* went to camp last year, and all my big sisters have gone to Camp Mohawk. And now Faye is a CIT and Autumn is a *counsellor*."

"Well, *my* big sister is a *junior* CIT," said Margo.

"I've never heard of such a thing. . . . And give me back my brush!"

By now, everyone, even Connie our counsellor, was watching what was going on. I decided to show them what a good CIT I could be. I would solve the problem and stop the fight. I marched over to Tara's bunk, bent down, rifled through her knapsack, and came up with a brush that was identical to Margo's. "This yours?" I asked Tara.

"Yes," she admitted.

The other campers returned to their unpacking. The fight was over. But Margo and Nancy Dawes seemed in awe of Tara.

Tara glowered at Margo and then at me. Faye glowered at me, too.

What had gone wrong? I'd solved the hairbrush problem, hadn't I?

Connie saw that we four CITs looked like being three against one. (Three against me.) "Have you all unpacked?" she asked us.

We nodded.

51

"Then why don't you sit out on the porch and get to know each other?"

Obediently, we filed out of the door in our sweet little Camp Mohawk outfits. Randi, Faye, and Julie squeezed themselves on to a big porch swing. (Wooden, of course.)

There was no room for me.

I sat on the steps. I thought of sitting with my back to them but decided not to. So I sat sideways, leaning against a post. I thought about how brave I'd been during the Tara-Margo fight. Where had that confidence come from? It was a little scary. The confidence wasn't me. And now it was fading away. My usual shyness was slipping over me like a veil.

What am I doing here? I wondered. I don't want to be sitting with these girls. They don't like me. And I'm not sure I like them. I want one of my friends—Kristy or Dawn or Claudia or Stacey or somebody.

I felt tears pricking at my eyes. But I couldn't cry. Not at the cabin. Not in front of the girls. This was neither the place nor the time to fall apart.

"So you have a boyfriend. Logan," Julie said to me.

I just nodded.

"Is he nice?"

"Mm-hmm," I could barely speak.

"I bet you don't have a boyfriend," said Faye tauntingly.

52

I didn't answer her.

"See?" Faye went on. "She doesn't have a boyfriend. What a liar."

If I put on some bracelets and earrings, would that make a difference? Would the girls believe me then?

Through a window of the cabin I suddenly heard Tara's voice. ". . . and on Fridays, we have fried snake for dinner. You have to go out and catch your own snake. Then you fry it up and—"

"Ugh, ugh! I'm going to be sick!" Margo cried. "It's disgusting!"

Tara laughed. She sounded satisfied.

I dashed into the cabin in case Margo really was going to be sick.

I had landed in a cabin full of troublemakers, I thought. I didn't know what to do about Tara the Terror just yet. But I had an idea about how to handle the CITs. I would just have to prove to them that Logan existed.

I would show them that I was as sophisticated as they were.

Saturday

Dear Dad and Jeff,

Well, I'm at camp again. It's been a while since I've lived in a cabin with a crowd of other girls and had to wear the same clothes day after day. (Well, not exactly the same clothes, but you know what I mean.) Anyway, I think Camp Mohawk is going to be a lot of fun. The campers in my cabin are eleven years old, and they seem a really nice group. The other CIT is nice, too, and so is our counsellor. What more can I say? I'm all set for fun and adventure!

Love and Sunshine,
Dawn

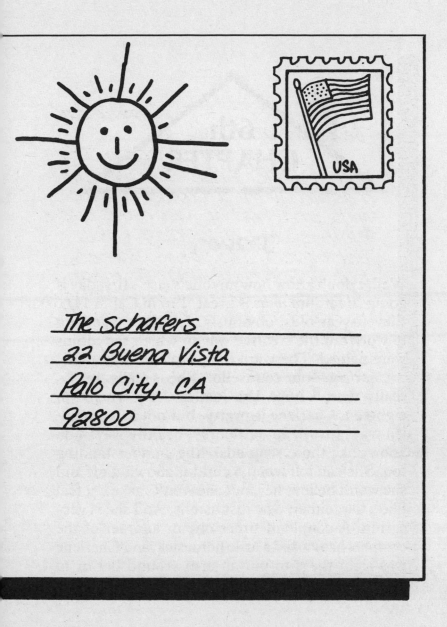

The schafers
22 Buena Vista
Palo City, CA
92800

6th
CHAPTER

Dawn

Well, I don't know how anyone's else's first day is going so far, but *mine* is great. I'm in Cabin 11A. Eleven-year-olds, obviously. It didn't take long to work out the creative way in which the cabins were named. These are the people in my cabin:

Charlene—our counsellor. She is really, really, really nice. I hope I'm just like her when I'm eighteen. Charlene is pretty, but not in a model-ish way. Just in an outdoorsy, healthy way. You know, like those soap ads? She's understanding too. She can tell when a child is showing off and she won't believe her, but she won't make her feel like a liar, either. She just listens. And she is very caring. A couple of times one or another of the campers has looked a little homesick, and Charlene was right there to put an arm around her or to assure her that homesickness isn't fatal. (Charlene has a sense of humour, too.)

Amy—the other CIT. She went to Camp Mohawk last summer, but she doesn't have as much camping experience as I have. She's not exactly pretty, but she's not bad-looking, either. Her eyes are sort of close together and her nose is pointy, so she looks a little like a bird. But she's got beautiful red-blonde hair (more red than blonde) and perfect skin. I think she's very clever.

Rachel—a camper who has been going to Mohawk since she was six, the youngest you can come here. Rachel will be staying all summer. She talks very fast and tries to be friendly to everyone, which is nice, but I have a feeling she thinks her parents dump her here every summer so that they can get rid of her and her brother (he's across the lake) and have time to themselves.

Shari (short for Sharilyn)—a funny camper. Actually, she's crazy, but everyone likes her a lot. I bet she's the class clown in school. Shari likes practical jokes, but I don't think she'd do anything that would hurt someone. She brought along a book of jokes and riddles and has been reading them aloud all afternoon. This is the only thing I have to say about the jokes, except that most of them are funny: If I repeated them to my mum or my grandparents, I would be in trouble.

Freddie (short for I don't know what, since she won't tell us)—came up on the bus from New York City. Freddie seems a little more sophisticated than the other girls. I mean, she looks older and knows about things the other girls have never even heard of, such as how to store your fur coat in the summer and dining *al fresco*, which means "outdoors". But she gets along well with everyone, laughs at Shari's jokes, listens to Rachel even when she's talking a hundred miles an hour, etc.

Donna—has gigantic ideas and plans. I think a psychiatrist would describe her plans as "grandiose". For instance, as soon as we reached our cabin, she said, "Hey, let's put our things away later, go and raid the kitchen instead, and have a hot dog feast by the lake. We'll invite 11B to join us, only they have to come in their pyjamas." Donna and Shari get along well and have decided to share a pair of bunks.

Caryn (pronounced Car-in)—has a million boyfriends, if you can believe her. She came all the way from Princeton, New Jersey. (Her dad, who grew up around here, went to Camp Mohawk when *he* was a child and wanted Caryn to come, too. Luckily, she loves it.) Caryn tells tall tales. We all know it, and none of us cares. She and Freddie are going to share a pair of bunks.

Heather—Now here is the exception to the rule. The rule of our campers, that is. Heather is everything the other campers aren't, and isn't anything they are. She is very, very quiet and barely spoke twice all afternoon. In fact, I think she spoke exactly twice. When Charlene called Heather's name in roll-call, Heather said, "Here." And when Rachel got stuck without someone to share a pair of bunks with her and was forced to ask Heather to share hers, Heather said, "Okay."

Heather is a teeny bit on the plump side, as if, at eleven, she still has baby fat. She wears glasses. She parts her fine brown hair in the middle and lets it hang across her face—so that she can hide behind it, I think. (But I had a look at her face once and she's very pretty.) Heather spent all afternoon lying on her bed (the bottom bunk; Rachel claimed the top one), writing in a diary and then reading *Anne of Green Gables*. I can't tell if she's shy or frightened or stuck-up. Charlene thinks she's just quiet.

When the nine of us first arrived at Cabin 11A, Charlene told us to unpack before we did anything else, and showed us where to put our things. That meant we had to choose someone to share a pair of bunks with us straight away. For Amy and me, this was no problem. CITs have to stick together, so we shared.

I wondered what it would have been like if any of us club members had ended up as co-CITs, Mary Anne and I in the same cabin, for instance. I think it would have been fun, but not as broadening. "Broadening" is a word Mum has been using a lot lately. She's forever talking about the need to broaden experiences, especially her own. The only two members of the Babysitters Club who ended up together were Mal and Jessi, and they aren't really CITs. They're right next door in 11B. I think it's a good thing they ended up together and also a good thing I'm not their CIT.

Anyway, as 11A unpacked, I listened to what was going on around me.

"Oh, no!" exclaimed Rachel. "A spider! There's a spider. It's over there on that wall by the knothole. Someone kill it! Quick!"

"How can you see that spider from all the way across the cabin?" asked Freddie. "That's amazing."

"I have bionic vision," replied Rachel. "Honestly I do. You know normal eyesight is twenty over twenty? And poor eyesight could be two hundred over twenty? Well, mine's twenty fifteen. That means I can see from twenty feet what most people can only see from fifteen feet. Or something like that. I could have all those numbers mixed up. I really could. But the main thing is, my eyesight's incredible. Once I was— Aargh! Aargh! The spider's moving! Honestly. Someone get rid of it. Please!"

Rachel was making everyone jumpy. A couple of girls let out little shrieks. I'm not particularly fond of spiders, but I tried to stay calm. Shari threw a trainer at the wall, which missed the spider by a mile. The shoe landed on Heather's head. Heather appeared not to notice, and Donna giggled at her.

"Hey, everyone," said Freddie, "the spider's heading for the knothole. I think it's going to crawl outside."

"Clever spider," I said.

"Does that knothole go all the way through the wall to the outside?" squeaked Rachel. "Then the spider could come back *in*. *And* we're going to freeze at night."

"Well, the cabins aren't exactly heated, anyway," Charlene pointed out. "And you Mohawkers have your lovely teepee sweaters to wear if we have cold weather."

Everyone laughed. Even Heather. Are "ha-ha" words? If so, then I counted wrong. Heather spoke three times this afternoon.

"My boyfriend," said Caryn, "told me the cabins on the other side of the lake are equipped with heating *and* air-conditioning."

"He's lying," said Donna. "They've only got microwaves."

"Who's your boyfriend?" asked Freddie.

"He'd better not be lying," replied Caryn, "and my boyfriend is Steve Heineman."

"Have you got a boyfriend, Heather?" Shari asked suddenly.

We had just about finished our unpacking and were sitting around our cabin, mostly on the top bunks, since it's so hard to see from the bottom ones. It's like being in a cave. But Heather was lying on her bottom bunk. She was in the diary-writing phase of the afternoon. I looked at her thoughtfully. She reminded me an awful lot of Mallory. Only in a good way.

"No," said Heather. "I haven't got a boy-friend." (Okay, she said four things this after-noon.)

Shari giggled, but then she began to tell one of her unrepeatable jokes, so I wasn't sure whether she was laughing at Heather, or at the punchline she knew was coming up.

After four of Shari's jokes, Charlene said, "Anyone who wants to go exploring now is allowed to. Free afternoon. Go and look at the stables, the lake, anything."

I thought Cabin 11A would come crashing down as everyone jumped off the top bunk beds and ran to the door. Charlene and Amy followed the campers outside. But I hung back. Heather was still lying on her bunk, writing.

"Aren't you going out?" I asked her.

Heather shook her head solemnly. "Charlene said anyone who *wants* to go, can go. I don't want to go. I'd rather stay here."

"Why did you come to camp, Heather?" I couldn't resist asking.

"Because my parents made me. They thought it would be a good experience." (Broadening, probably.)

62

"And what do you think?"

"I'm willing to experiment." Heather looked back at her diary. (So she said quite a few things this afternoon. I was exaggerating a bit before.)

"Are you sure you don't want to come outside? I'll walk around with you," I offered.

"That's okay," said Heather. "Really. Thanks, but you go ahead."

So I did. I thought a lot about Heather that afternoon.

Saturday night

Dear Laine,

How's New York? Are you surprised to hear that I miss you and it already? well, I do. There is absolutely no use for credit cards up here. What we could do with is a hospital. Did you know that six-year-olds get ill a lot? I don't know why I didn't realize it before, what with all the babysitting I do. I suppose I've just never spent so much time with so many six-year-olds. Also, six-year-olds are loud. I will have to demonstrate the difference between "indoor voices" and "outdoor voices" to them.

Love,
Your frazzled friend,
Stacey

Laine Cummings

The Dakota

72nd and Central Park West

New York, NY 10000

7th CHAPTER

Stacey

Okay, all of you, I've read your notebook entries, so I know how your afternoons went. There were a few differences between yours and mine. For one thing, *your* campers could unpack for themselves. Mine couldn't. They need a lot more help with everything. I suppose that's to be expected.

Barbara, our counsellor, Joanne, the other CIT in our cabin, and I went from bunk to bunk, helping the little children unpack. It seemed that each time we got to a new child, we got to a new illness, too.

Yuck. I can't stand sickness, maybe because of my diabetes, and because I've spent a fair amount of time in hospitals over the past few years. So I started off by helping Karen Brewer unpack. I've known Karen since our family moved to Stoneybrook, and Karen is usually healthy.

Today I discovered something new, though. She may be healthy, but put her in with a lot of six-year-olds and she's loud. Shrill, actually. I think she just gets a little overexcited. Also, it was her first day at camp, and her first time away from home alone. So I tried to be understanding when she said (shrieked), "Stacey! I'm at camp! Can you believe it? Hey look, all of you." (Calling to everyone in the cabin.) "I'm a Martian. Here's my Martian face. And here's my Martian voice. Eeeeeeee!"

Whoa! I had to settle Karen down. She was giving me a headache. And she was exciting the other children. "Would you do me a big favour?" I said to Karen. "Would you be my helper, and go to each camper and make sure she's got everything she came with? If anything's missing, report back to me immediately."

Karen grinned proudly and was off and running.

I moved on to the next camper. "I've got a sore throat," she said.

"Hey, Stacey," called Barbara, the counsellor, from across the cabin. "Do you know what conjunctivitis looks like?"

Oh, for goodness' sake! I dashed over to Barbara and looked into the pixie face of a smiling redhead. She didn't seem sick at all. But one eye was about the colour of her hair.

"Does it itch?" I asked her.

"Mm-hmm," she said, reaching for her eye.

I pulled her hand back. "Don't touch it," I said. "That'll make it worse." (I sounded exactly like my mother.)

"And now," spoke up a little voice behind me, "you'd better wash your hand, Shtashey."

I turned around to see who the lisper was. Standing with her hands on her hips and brown hair flowing down her back (her hair was so long she could sit on it) was a cheeky-looking camper.

"Why, Nonie?" I asked, pleased with myself for remembering her name.

"Because if Valerie'sh hand hash touched her eye, then she hash germs on her hand, sho now you probly have germs on *your* hand and if *you* touch *your* eye *you'll* get conjunctivitis, too."

Great. Just great, I thought.

"You seem to know a lot about conjunctivitis," I said to Nonie.

"I have three shishters and a brother," she replied. "We've all gone to Camp Mohawk. I know everything about big familiesh, everything about pashing shicknishesh around, and *everything* about camp. If you've got a queshtion, I can ansher it. Oh, yeah. One more thing. I know everything about playing jokesh on people, too." Nonie looked meaningfully at the other little girls.

"Everything?" repeated Karen.

"Everything."

68

"I've got two big stepbrothers," Karen told Nonie, "and one of them—his name his Sam—well, *he* knows everything about playing jokes. He's an expert."

"Maybe, maybe not," replied Nonie.

Karen and Nonie became involved in a joke-playing discussion.

I became involved in worrying. In our cabin, we had a sore throat. We had conjunctivitis. However, the camp does have an infirmary. It's here to see to sore throats and conjunctivitis. So Barbara walked Valerie and Monique (the girl with the sore throat) over to the infirmary. She left Joanne and me in charge of the rest of the campers.

My worrying continued. Nonie was still telling practical-joke stories. "Hot Shtuff Chewing Gum," she was saying. "It burnsh your mouth out! And once my oldesht shishter, when she wash here at camp, she took another camper's underwear and ran it up the flagpole!"

The campers giggled delightedly.

But all I could think of was Betsy Sobak. She's the child Claudia sat for who was the champion practical joker of the world and ended up doing a trick that landed Claud in hospital with a broken leg.

The afternoon wore on. Barbara returned with Valerie and Monique, ointment for Valerie's eye, tablets for Monique's throat, and instructions to watch both girls closely to make sure they didn't get any worse.

Dinnertime. I could feel butterflies in my stomach. Not because I was nervous about eating in a hall, or about helping to watch six-year-olds as *they* ate, but because of the food. I didn't expect it to be good, of course. School dinners never are, so why should camp food be any different? It's hard to maintain quality when you're cooking for hundreds. You probably have to cut corners here and there in order to get vats of soup instead of just one pan.

No, I was worried about my diet. Mum and Dad had had three chats with Mrs Means before camp started. They had told her what I can and can't eat, and that I have to take in a certain number of calories every day. Therefore, if part of the meal is something with sugar or syrup in it, I can't eat it, *but* I can't skip it, either. I need something non-sugary to replace it.

Mrs Means said about seventy-five times that she'd see that I was given only meals I could eat. After all, no one wanted to see me go into insulin shock.

So imagine my surprise this evening when I sat down to a meal of meat loaf, a potato, salad with honey dressing, and a chocolate biscuit. The meat and potato were fine. The salad and the biscuit weren't.

Now what? I couldn't eat just the meat and

potato. That wasn't enough, and besides, I'm supposed to have *extremely* balanced meals. I tried to catch Claudia's eye across the room, but that was impossible. She was busy with her group of children, and in between us were a bunch of slaphappy, first-day campers. They were shouting, jumping in and out of their seats, and throwing food around. One girl tossed a biscuit in the air—and I never saw it come down, although it must have eventually.

With a huge sigh, I excused myself from the table and carried my plate into the kitchen.

I nearly crashed into a cook.

"What are you doing in here?" he demanded.

"I can't eat some of these things," I told him.

"Listen," he replied, "you get what you get. I know the food's not gourmet, but you don't see anyone else coming back here just because this isn't like home cooking."

"But I'm diabetic." I was trying to explain what that meant when Mrs Means came in. She and the cook and I had a talk. When I left the kitchen a little while later, I was carrying a plate of meat, potato, an apple, and a sugar-free whole-wheat muffin—on a clean plate, with no traces of honey.

Mrs Means assured me there would be no further problems, but I still had to face my campers, their questions, and a lot of stares.

"How come you get shpecial food, Shtashey?"

asked you-know-who.

"I want an apple, too," said Monique. But she couldn't have one. They were for tomorrow's lunch, and there had to be enough to go around. I felt awful.

Somehow, though, we made it through dinner. It was time for a group sing-song that was to be held in Mohawk Meadow around the flagpole. Mrs Means had said earlier that it was a nice way to get all the campers together, but I think it was really just an opportunity for her to make some announcements to us. She did that first. *Then* we sang.

The announcements were pretty much what I expected. She reminded us about camp rules and safety measures. Then she started on health hazards, which didn't thrill me, what with the conjunctivitis and the sore throat. She warned us about poison ivy and poison oak, about not eating toadstools and berries, and that sort of thing. She added that there were no snakes in the lake—and I heard both Mary Anne and Jessi scream at the very thought of snakes!

Then Mrs Means told us about something called Lyme disease. "You get it from ticks," she told us. "Not the larger ticks you often see on dogs or cats, but tiny ticks—about the size of the full-stop at the end of a sentence, so they're very hard to see. Lyme disease is relatively new. It's only become a problem in the last few years, but now you can get it in many states of the country. And New York is one of them. It's easy to pick up the ticks in woods or fields, or from animals. Lyme disease can be serious, so check yourselves carefully for ticks. And if you notice a round, red, spreading rash anywhere on your body, or begin to feel achy and tired, as if you have flu, go to the infirmary at once."

I was scared to death.

I was also tired and cold and getting bitten by mosquitoes, so I moved back to the edge of the crowd of campers and settled into a comfortable patch of leaves. Maybe the mosquitoes would leave me alone there.

Mrs Means began the first song *"Oh, it ain't gonna rain no more, no more. It ain't gonna rain no more. How in the heck can I wash my neck, if it ain't gonna rain no more?"*

Funny song. I grinned and settled into my leafy nest. Maybe camp wouldn't be so bad after all.

  Sunday

Dear Claire,
   Hi, there! How does it feel to be an only
child? You have Mummy and Daddy and the
hamster all to yourself. Do you miss your
brothers and sisters? I miss you. Camp is
fun. We live in cabins. We sleep in bunk beds,
just like the ones in the boys' room at home.
Last night all the campers gathered at a
place called Mohawk Meadow and sang songs.
We learned a funny one about someone who
couldn't wash his neck because there was no
rain water! Maybe next year you'll come to
Camp Mohawk, too

                        I love you.
                        Your sister,
                            Mallory

Claire Pike

134 Slate Street

Stoneybrook, CT 06800

8th CHAPTER

Mallory

It was funny to wake up this morning in a tiny bed that wasn't mine, and to know that Jessi was in the bed below me. I turned over and gazed at the things on the three shelves lining my bunk. Then I turned over again and looked round our cabin. My cabin-mates were starting to wake up. They stirred in that last, light sleep of the morning, or coughed, or murmured things that were probably the ends of dreams.

I looked at my watch. It was 6:45. We would be woken up at seven. How, I didn't know. I was pretty sure it wouldn't be a camp-sized alarm clock.

I leaned over my bed and peered down at Jessi. She was lying on her front, reading *Misty of Chincoteague* for about the eighteenth time.

"PSST!" I hissed. "Jessi!"

Jessi rolled over and looked up at me. She grinned. "Morning."

"Morning," I replied.

"SHHHHHHH!" said someone else. "We've still got fifteen minutes."

Help! I thought. Jessi and I can't do anything right.

I shrugged at Jessi and pulled myself back up to the top bunk, where I opened my copy of *Stormy, Misty's Foal* and began reading that for about the eighteenth time.

I was at a really exciting part of the story when: "ATTENTION, ALL CAMPERS AND COUNSELLORS! ATTENTION, ALL CAMPERS AND COUNSELLORS! GOOD MORNING. TODAY IS SUNDAY." (Groan.) "BREAKFAST WILL BE SERVED IN HALF AN HOUR. THE MENU IS WAFFLES, BACON, AND ORANGE JUICE. HAVE A NICE DAY!"

I pictured Mrs Means wearing a smiley face.

Since Jessi and I had been awake for a while, we immediately snapped our books shut and pulled clean teepee outfits off our shelves. I jumped down from my bed, and Jessi and I began to change our clothes.

"The twins are at it again," I heard someone in an upper bunk whisper to someone in a lower bunk. I think it was Mary to Mary.

"Yeah, goody-two-shoes," added Mandi sleepily.

"Stop that!" said Autumn, from behind her curtain.

I looked around. Jessi and I were the only ones up and moving.

"But there's only half an hour until breakfast," I whispered nervously to Jessi. "We don't want to be late."

One of the Marys snorted. (How had she even heard me?)

Jessi linked arms with me. "Let's go," she said resolutely, and we headed for the washrooms to wash our faces and brush our teeth.

"Oreos," Maureen said as we left the cabin.

I didn't know what she meant, but I did hear Autumn say sharply, "Maureen, I don't want to hear you say that again. Not ever."

"Oreos?" I repeated to Jessi.

Jessi scowled. "Yeah, a really nice word," she said sarcastically, "meaning someone whose skin is black, but who acts like a white person. Get it? Black on the outside, white on the inside, like a chocolate-covered Oreo biscuit."

"But Maureen said Oreos," I pointed out. "I'm not black."

"I know. Either she's really stupid" (I giggled), "or she meant that somehow you and I together make up an Oreo biscuit because we stick together so much," said Jessi.

"An Oreo biscuit with one part gone because my brother Nicky has bitten it off, dipped it in

78

milk, and eaten it," I said.

Jessi and I laughed at that, and also at Maureen for not even knowing what an Oreo is. She tried to insult us and she used the word all wrong. We were in a pretty good mood by the time the rest of our cabin-mates dragged themselves into the washrooms.

"There are the twins," said Mary Travis loudly.

"Where?" I replied.

Mary just stared.

"Oh, *us*?" I asked. "You mean the Oreos? I thought you said yesterday that we don't look alike enough to be twins."

Mary blushed, then turned on the water in one of the basins and began washing her face. No one else said anything to Jessi or me, so we left.

We were on our own.

Now maybe this sounds as though we were going to have a bad day. No. Not at all. We were going to have a great day.

That was because later, Jessi and I had our first chance to work with the eight-year-olds on their dance routine for Parents' Day. Until we met the children, we weren't sure whether we were getting Cabin 8A or Cabin 8B. We got Cabin 8B, the cabin with Becca and Charlotte in it!

Oh, boy! First of all, both of them have terrible stage fright, especially Becca. Secondly, Becca has never danced in her life. She has two left feet. How Jessi can be so talented and coordinated, and Becca so untalented and uncoordinated, is beyond me, but that's the way things are. Thirdly, Charlotte is homesick and cries a lot.

(I know this doesn't sound like much fun, but as usual, I'm getting ahead of myself.)

Early on Sunday afternoon, Jessi and I walked over to the recreation hall, where we were supposed to meet the 8B girls. The rec. hall is a large (wooden) building that is empty except for a ping-pong table and an air hockey game. The rest of it is used for watching films or playing games on rainy days, for parties, for dances for the CITs and counsellors, and for rehearsals. That's what Autumn told us.

The eight-year-olds arrived at the rec. hall just as we did.

"Jessi, Jessi, Jessi!" cried Becca, and flung herself at her sister.

"Mal, Mal, Mal!" cried Charlotte, and flung herself at me. I'm sure she really wanted Stacey, but I was a good second choice.

Jessi and I and the six children walked into the rec. hall. The children sat on the floor. Jessi and I stood in front of them. I looked helplessly at Jessi. What were we supposed to do? I've never been a teacher. And what I know about dancing you could fit in a thimble.

But Jessi just said easily, "Hi, I'm Jessi Ramsey.

I'm Becca's sister. And this is my friend Mallory. Guess what? You've got a really important job. You're going to perform a dance on Parents' Day. Don't worry if you think you can't dance. We'll teach you. I've had lots of ballet lessons. Besides, anyone can dance. It's just another way of expressing yourselves, like talking."

"Jessi dances on *toe*," Becca spoke up importantly. "She's been *in* ballets *on* stage in front of hundreds of people."

"Oooh," breathed the girls, clearly impressed.

"Now, we're not going to do just ballet," Jessi continued. "It's too hard without ballet shoes. We're going to learn a little jazz and throw some aerobics and acrobatics in, too. It'll be fun, I promise. Lots of jumping around."

"Will an awful lot of people be watching us?" asked Charlotte in a wavery voice. Becca seemed worried, too.

My heart almost broke. Homesickness and stage fright. What a terrible combination. I sat next to Charlotte on the floor and put my arm around her. "I don't know, Char," I told her. "I honestly don't. For now, let's just try dancing. It'll be fun."

"Okay, everybody. On your feet!" Jessi called cheerfully.

We stood up, Charlotte wiping tears from her eyes.

"Mal, you stay with the children," Jessi said to

81

me, "and give them a hand when they need it. Or a foot. I'll stand here and lead things."

That was fine with me.

"Warm-ups!" announced Jessi. "And one and two and three and four. And one and two and three and four." She touched her knees, her toes, her knees again, and then her hips and she counted.

Not one of the kids could get the sequence right. Half of them were touching their knees while the other half were touching their toes. And Charlotte kept putting her hands in the air instead of on her hips.

"Ahem," said Jessi, "let's try something else. Everyone curl into a ball on the floor. Now very slowly uncurl yourselves and stand up. Pretend you're flowers growing."

The girls curled up. Then everyone stood slowly, except for Becca, who shot to her feet.

"*Becca*," complained Jessi.

"I'm a sunflower," said Becca. "Sunflowers grow fast. Don't they?"

"Yes."

"And you always say that a good dancer is creative. So—so I was being creative."

Jessi sighed, then smiled. Becca managed to look both proud and worried. She knew she was not a good dancer, but she wanted very badly to please her big sister.

The "rehearsal" went on for forty-five minutes.

Girls crashed into each other. They fell down. They mixed up their rights and their lefts.

They giggled hysterically, even Charlotte.

So did Jessi and I. We were having a great time. But what on earth were we going to do for our show on Parents' Day?

Sunday afternoon

Dear Mum and Watson,

Gosh, am I tired. How did you two ever raise so many children? I think I'll just have one child when I grow up. Or maybe two. Or three. But no more than five or six. Anyway, why am I tired? Not because I'm in a cabin with six eight-year-old campers, but because I'm in a cabin with Charlotte Johanssen. She is so homesick. I feel really sorry for her. I'm not sure she's going to last the two weeks here, although Becca Ramsey will be pretty unhappy if she doesn't. Don't get me wrong. Camp is fun, too. I went swimming in the lake this morning, and I also rode a horse!

Love,
Kristy

Mr. and Mrs. Watson Brewer

1210 McLelland Road

Stoneybrook, CT 06800

9th CHAPTER

Kristy

I wrote a postcard to Mum and Watson and everything I told them was true. I'm having fun at camp and Charlotte is homesick, but she's even more homesick than I let on. Also I feel a bit left out with the other CITs in Cabins 8B and 8A. There aren't problems, exactly. The CITs haven't been mean to me. Not at all. They couldn't be nicer. It's just that I'm so different from them. Oh, all right, I'll be honest, it's that I'm exactly their age, but I seem so much younger. That's how I felt compared to Stacey and Claudia when the Babysitters Club first began. And that's how I feel now compared to almost all of the club members. The big difference is that I know my friends so well. I feel comfortable with them. So the difference doesn't matter. But I don't know the CITs.

The CITs are Lauren, Izzie, and Tansy. (Tansy is my co-CIT.) The counsellors are Jo and Naomi. Jo is my counsellor. Everyone knows Jo. She's the only person at Camp Mohawk who actually *has* a mohawk hairstyle. The front half is red and the back half is blue. (Well, they were at first.) The second we got to our cabins Old Meanie turned up and said Jo would have to have her hair cut, because such hair is not fitting for a role model. But Jo said no, absolutely not. She said her hair was *her hair* and she could do whatever she wanted with it. Later, though, she took a shower and the red and blue washed out. It turned out the colours were only sprayed on. Jo is clever. I think she did that on purpose. Now Old Meanie feels she made Jo tone down her hair, when all Jo wanted in the first place was the mohawk. She didn't care about the colours.

Anyway, back to the CITs. The very first thing Tansy said to me as were were walking from the buses to Cabin 8B (Charlotte clinging desperately to my hand), was, "My name's Tansy. I know it's a weird name. It comes from a Greek word meaning immortal, and it's also the name of a flower. So I don't mind the name at all. It's an important one."

All I could say was, "I looked my name up in a book once and I couldn't find it." I felt really daft.

Tansy's reply was, "I need new nail polish."

After we had reached the cabins and unpacked,

we four CITs took a break. We sat on the steps in front, leaning against posts so that we could face each other. Before anyone had opened her mouth, I could tell how different I was from them. There we were, all wearing teepee shirts and shorts and socks. But Tansy, Lauren, and Izzie were wearing smart-looking white lace-up trainers on their feet, and I was wearing blue shoes with velcro straps. I almost always wear lace-up running shoes, but just before we left for camp, I saw these shoes and bought them. I thought they looked really fashionable.

I suppose I was wrong.

Tansy and Lauren were wearing nail polish. I wasn't.

Izzie was wearing lipstick and had pierced ears. I wasn't and didn't.

Tansy, Lauren, and Izzie were wearing eye makeup. I wasn't.

The first words out of Lauren's mouth, after a huge sigh, were, "I miss my boyfriend already."

"Me too," said Izzie and Tansy with equally huge sighs.

The three of them looked at me.

I paused. Then I said, "I miss Bart."

The girls looked relieved.

"He's a friend of mine," I added, not wanting to lie.

"Your *boy*friend?" asked Lauren.

I shook my head.

Lauren glanced at Izzy, Izzy glanced at Tansy, Tansy glanced at both of them and then looked at me.

"Do you have a real boyfriend?" asked Tansy.

"No. Just some friends who are boys."

"You know," said Izzy, leaning towards me, "you would look so pretty if you cut your hair a little and got rid of your fringe."

As Izzy leaned over, I caught sight of a bra strap peeping out from under the shoulder of her teepee shirt. Oh, lord! Suddenly I was sure Tansy and Lauren were wearing bras, too. I wasn't, of course. Have I ever? Furthermore, I want to point out that I'm the shortest of the CITs. I'm the shortest Babysitters Club member, too. Won't I *ever* grow up?

Well, anyway, soon Tansy, Lauren, and Izzie were all examining me and making comments: "Blusher would help."; "What other shoes did she bring?"; "I think plum nail polish would go best with her eyes."

It was as if I weren't even there; as if I were just a spot on a slide under a microscope. I felt like an amoeba.

I also felt as though I was four years old. Was that how Charlotte was feeling?

That night was the group sing-song though, and I really had fun. And today, the other CITs and I went swimming and rode horses. In between, however . . . Charlotte.

Oh, she is a problem. At dinner last night (if you could call it "dinner"), she dropped her fork on the floor. For Charlotte, that was bad enough. She was so embarrassed by that one little incident (and believe me, people were dropping things right and left, so it was no big deal), that by the time she'd found it under our table, she was crying. Then, as she straightened up, practically from out of nowhere came one of those chocolate biscuits. It dropped on to her head from the ceiling! Poor Charlotte.

I took her out of the hall to clean her up. When we had finished, she tried to tell me something. But she was crying awfully hard. What I heard was, "I-I-I-I-I-I-I-wahhhhh g-o-m-e!"

"You want to what?" I said, kneeling down next to her. We were in the cloakroom in Mrs Meanie's office.

"Gome," Char replied. (Hiccup.)

"Gome? Gome? . . . *Oh*. Go home?"

Charlotte nodded.

Mrs Means let us use her phone. (There are hardly any phones here. The only other one is in the infirmary. There are also two phones on the boys' side.)

After Charlotte's mother had worked out what "gome" meant, she talked to Charlotte for a long time. At least I think she did, because Charlotte was quiet for a long time. Dr Johanssen must also have told Charlotte she could phone any time she wanted (Charlotte called again an hour later), and that if she really wanted, she *could* come home. I think Charlotte might have done that, except for Becca. She couldn't desert her friend. She did, however, spend the night with me. I mean, literally. In my sleeping bag.

The next morning, Jo was in charge of the campers and that was when she found out everything Charlotte's afraid of. Horses, swimming in the lake, boats . . . Charlotte quite enjoyed a dance rehearsal with Jessi and Mallory early in the afternoon, but later, she wouldn't agree to anything except archery. This was because no one else wanted to arch (or whatever it's called) and there's no archery instructor anyway. Just some old bows and arrows and targets. Guess who was put in charge of Charlotte? Me. I wanted to go swimming, which was what practically everyone else was doing, but I didn't want to hurt Charlotte's feelings, and besides, as a CIT, watching the campers is my job.

We set up a target in a field that no one was using (since they were all swimming). I showed Charlotte how to put on her wrist guard, how to position the bow and arrow, how to aim, and thought, Good thing we had that silly archery class in gym this year.

Charlotte took aim. She pulled the arrow back. She let it fly.

WHOOSH!

As the arrow was heading towards the target, a little child stepped on to the other side of the field. She was heading for the lake, wearing a swimsuit and trying to walk in flippers. Suddenly she tripped and fell.

"Aarghhh!" shrieked Charlotte. "Aarghhh! Aarghhh! I shot her!"

"Char, you did not. She's walking away. And, look—you hit the target."

Charlotte wasn't listening to me. Finally I packed everything up, took Char back to our cabin, and began reading *A Morgan for Melinda* to her, which I found on Becca's bunk. It's a horse story. I thought maybe she'd learn not to be afraid of horses. But what I was wondering was whether Char should be at Camp Mohawk at all.

                              Tuesday
Dear mum and dad,

   Hi how are you? Me just fin. Camp is
realy fun. I have riden a horse and swam
in a lake. But mosty I hav been in the art
and crafts cabin. As you can imergine. I'am
working on potery but also on some
niddlework. Tell Mimi now I know why
she and Mary ann like it so much. I hop
she teaches me to knit when I som home
if she can. Guess what Maly bradock is
teaching her cabin-mates how to do sign langage
it was her own idea.

                              Love,
   P.S. I met a   Claudia
gorgeous boy, realy
gorgeous and he's
japanese!

Mr and Mrs John Kishi

58 Bradford CT

Stoneybrook, Conn 06800

10th CHAPTER

Claudia

Well, I finished writing to my parents. I told them about riding and swimming and arts and crafts. I told them about Haley teaching the other children sign language. I didn't tell them that I'm spending my money in the canteen on M&Ms, liquorice sticks, Snickers Bars, Walnut Whips, etc. I'm in seventh heaven. ("Seventh heaven" is something Mum says, but I wonder what it means. I know it means "happy", but . . . where are the other six heavens? Oh, well.)

I also didn't tell my parents the whole story about the boy I met. But let me go back to the beginning of the day first, starting with breakfast. Breakfast was biscuits left over from Saturday, fried eggs that slid around on our plates, and black things that might have been muffins, but it was hard to tell. The meal was simply awful. So afterwards, I ran immediately to the camp shop. I was desperate. Sally, the other CIT, and Haley and Vanessa came with me.

We all had money in our pockets, we were starving, and we got there before the camp shop opened. My watch read 8:58. The canteen opens at nine. They are very precise.

Two counsellors, I think one was Autumn and I *know* the other was Mohawk Jo, were manning the campshop that morning. When they opened the sales window and found the four of us on the other side, practically drooling with hunger, they looked a little startled.

"How was breakfast?" asked Autumn.

Sally pretended to faint and I pretended to have to catch her.

"Food," Sally gasped. "Please. Food. . . . Real food."

"All right," said Jo, "what'll you have?"

"Hula Hoops," answered Sally.

"Crackers," replied Vanessa.

"Apple pie," said Haley.

"A Snickers Bar, a Walnut Whip, a Mars Bar, a bag of crisps, two packets of M&Ms, a tube of smarties, and some cheese biscuits." (That was me.)

Jo and Autumn stared.

"How do you stay so thin?" asked Jo.

"And how come your complexion's so good?" asked Autumn.

I shrugged. "Don't know. Just lucky, I

suppose. Or maybe good genes. I take after my grandmother."

Sally, Vanessa, Haley, and I raced back to our cabin, eating on the way.

"I've never been so hungry in my whole life," said Vanessa, cramming a third cracker into her mouth.

"The food here is terrible," agreed Haley, who hardly ever complains. "This apple pie is the best thing I've eaten since I got here. I wonder what the boys' food is like," she added, probably thinking about her brother on the other side of the lake.

"Just the same, I bet," said Sally, "but boys never notice the difference. They'd happily eat pond scum and gorilla feet, if they didn't know what it was. Or most of them would."

By the time we reached our cabin, everyone had finished their food but me. That was because I'd bought so much. All I'd eaten was a packet of M&Ms. I shoved everything else into a carrier bag on one of my shelves. Since I wasn't at home, I didn't have to bother to hide it.

That morning, our cabin went horseriding. It was fun! I haven't spent much time on horses, but this was nice. Of course, the horses weren't like rodeo horses, rearing on their hind legs and jumping around. They just walked along a well-worn path through the woods. Even so, by the time we got back to the stables, brushed the horses, helped muck out their stalls, and learned how to get them ready for the next riders, we were pretty disgusting-looking.

"You've got straw in your hair, Claudia!" said Jayme, dancing around like a pixie.

"And you've got dust on your nose," I replied, smiling.

"I think *I've* got dust *in* my nose," said Brandy, and sneezed.

When we reached our cabin, I made a beeline for the mirror.

I was worse than a mess, I was a *fright*! There really was straw in my hair. There was also dirt on my face, dust on my clothes and (ugh!) a caterpillar on my shoulder. I took the caterpillar off my shoulder and put it on Sally's pillow to see how she'd react.

Then I realized I smelled like horses and manure, but before I could shower I had to get the straw out of my hair.

That's just what I was doing when I heard footsteps on the cabin porch. Heavy footsteps.

"Hello?" called a boy's voice.

"Aarghh! Aarghh!" Everyone began screaming.

"I'm changing!" cried Leeann.

"I'm naked!" shrieked Vanessa.

"I'm Claudia," I said.

I knew exactly how bad I looked. I knew exactly how bad I smelled. But at least I was dressed.

I had turned away from the mirror

(wooden-framed) and stepped outside. A boy was standing on the porch. Two others were behind him on the path. When I came outside, the first boy backed away and joined his friends.

"Hi," he said. "I'm John and these are my friends." (He pointed to the other boys as he introduced them.) "We're CITs from across the lake. We're here to officially invite . . ."

John kept on talking, but I wasn't listening. All I could do was look at one of the other boys. He was gorgeous. Absolutely gorgeous—and incredible and wonderful. I'm sure of it.

And I think he's Japanese. Anyway, he's Asian. He has black, black hair and dark, almond-shaped eyes, and creamy skin like mine. His hair is kind of punk. The top part stands straight up. He must have to use mousse or something on it in the morning. That and his black trainers were about as punk as he could get at Camp Mohawk. The rest of his clothes were teepee variety.

I gazed at him.

He gazed at me.

John was still talking, but I wasn't listening, and I don't think the gorgeous boy was listening, either. At least not until we heard John say, "Well, see you a week from today."

The next thing I knew, the boys were gone.

"What? What?" I spluttered as I fled into the cabin.

I found my campers, Sally, and Meghan grinning at me.

"Woo—*oo*," said Brandy. "Claud and someone, sitting in a tree, K-I-S-S-I-N-G!"

"First comes love," added Leeann, "then comes—"

"What were they doing here?" I interrupted Leeann.

"What were they *do*ing here?" Sally repeated. "Weren't you listening? They were inviting us to the CIT Film Night next Tuesday, and the big CIT dance next Wednesday—on the boys' side."

"Across Lake Dekanunga?" I said.

Everyone laughed. Even me. I had said "Dekanunga" on purpose because I couldn't remember the real name of the lake. (I don't think anyone can.) That's a good way to get out of embarrassing situations—make a joke. I do that a lot in school.

"That boy," I said softly. "I have to meet him. Soon. But I don't even know his name."

"Hey," said Vanessa. "You really like him, don't you?"

I nodded.

"Love at first sight," said Haley dreamily.

The campers grew quiet and I realized that *they* had just realized that this was important to me. Very important.

"I've got to see him," I said again. "Before next Tuesday. I can't wait that long. Camp will

101

practically be over by then."

"We'll help you," spoke up Gail, who's our quietest camper. "We'll find him for you somehow."

"Yeah, we know there's a boy across the lake named John. We'll start with him," added Brandy.

"But there must be a thousand Johns over there," Jayme pointed out.

"And there are only two phones here: in the infirmary and in Old Meanie's office. How are we going to get in touch with the boys' side?" wondered Vanessa. (I could tell she liked the idea of a challenge, though.)

"Hey, not to change the subject," Meghan interrupted, and we turned our attention to our counsellor, "but Claudia, did you get the rest of John's message?"

"The rest of it?" I repeated, and everyone laughed.

"He and his friends had to go back across the lake, so John asked you and Sally to spread the word about the film and the dance to the other CITs here. Just tell every CIT you see about them, okay? Word will spread fast."

I nodded. Then I climbed on to my top bunk. I reached for my carrier bag, needing junk food badly. I was having an attack. I put my hand in the bag and felt around. Empty!

At that moment I heard two shrieks. One was a

shriek of laughter. That came from Vanessa Pike. The other was a shriek of horror. That came from Sally. I scrambled off my bunk bed, stepping on Sally's hand in the process.

"What's the matter?" I exclaimed.

"There's a worm on my bed!" she cried, and darted across the cabin, out of worm's way. (Oh, so *that's* what would happen if Sally found a caterpillar on her pillow.)

Nearby, Vanessa was laughing. I didn't have to ask her why, since she couldn't wait to tell me. "You know why you can't find your sweets?" she managed to say. "Because I hid them!"

This was Vanessa's idea of a big joke. The other campers thought it was pretty funny, too.

Vanessa produced the sweets. And I handed them round to everyone in my cabin, which was very generous of me. But to tell the truth, I was so intrigued by John's friend that I, Claudia Kishi, hardly cared about the size of my junk food supply.

Thursday
Dear Dad,
  Hi! How are you?
I'm fine. Camp's
fine. Gotta go.
    Bye. Love,
      Mary Anne
P.S. Pat Tigger
      for me.

Mr. Richard Spier
59 Bradford Court
Stoneybrook, CT
06800

11th CHAPTER

Mary Anne

I felt rather awful. I wrote a postcard to my father this morning, but I didn't have enough time to write a long one. So I wrote him a short one in big handwriting instead. I was too busy for postcards. This is why:

Dear Logan,
I miss you so much! I am counting the days until next Wednesday. This next week will seem like a year. I think of you and want to ~~men~~ swoon. Oh, to feel your arms around me at the dance! It has been too long since our last kiss.

I will be wearing the formal teepee wear, of course, and a yellow ribbon in my hair. What of you, my love? Will you wear your after-shave? If you were to bring me a yellow flower to match my ribbon, I would melt in your arms.

Love forever, kisses and hugs,
Your love-bunny,
Mary Anne xx oo

Logan has never in his life called me his love-bunny. I can't even imagine him doing that. And I've certainly never called *him my* love-bunny. We aren't like that.

I wrote that note for one reason only, and it hardly had anything to do with Logan. Not directly, anyway. I didn't even intend him to see it. It was written for Randi, my co-CIT, to discover. I wanted her and Faye and Julie, the CITs next-door in 7B, to read it. (I guessed that if Randi saw it, Faye and Julie would hear about it no more than one second later.)

Why did I want the girls to see the note? Because I wanted to prove just how sophisticated I was. I know, I know. It was stupid. And it doesn't even sound like me.

Since when did I care about things like that?

108

Since I got to Camp Mohawk and was more or less separated from my friends, that's when.

Anyway, what I did was to write that note yesterday and leave it on my bunk, hoping Randi would be the one to find it first—and she was. And, just as I suspected, she raced it over to Faye and Julie. I had taken Margo Pike and Nancy Dawes to the nature cabin to get them ready for a butterfly hunt they wanted to go on the next day. When we got back, Randi, Faye, and Julie were standing in the middle of the cabin, crowded around the note. Their heads jerked up as we came in, but they didn't look guilty, only smug.

"Um, Mary Anne," said Randi, sauntering over to me, "you left this on your bunk. I took it because I didn't want any of the campers to see it. I mean, really, what would they think? 'Love-bunny'?; 'Too long since our last kiss'?; 'Swooning'?"

Personally, I had a feeling our campers would be much more interested in whether they could sneak up to the windows of Old Meanie's cabin that evening and try to see what was on her TV, but I kept my mouth shut.

"So," said Faye, as the campers changed into their swimsuits (it was almost time for afternoon Open Swim), "how are you going to get this note to Logan?"

"Yeah, do you think you can do it fast enough for him to get you a yellow flower?"

"Maybe you should go at night," spoke up another voice. The CITs and I turned around.

Tara the Terror. *She* was more interested in Logan and me than in Mrs Means's TV. "But if you go at night," she continued slowly, "you'd have to get round bed-check. Somehow."

I sighed inwardly. Bed-check. I hate it. I think it says Old Meanie doesn't trust us. Imagine her and the head counsellors checking each and every bed at night to make sure they're occupied and no one is doing something she shouldn't be doing. Like taking a note around Lake Dukakis to her boyfriend.

"You can get round bed-check," said Julie. "Easy."

"Why not go tonight?" added Faye. "The sooner the better. You'll want the best yellow flower Logan can find."

I was trapped. I had to go. If I didn't, I'd look like a bigger baby than they already thought I was. But a trip around Lake Deckasaga? Alone? At night? I didn't even know the way. And I was not going to take a boat by myself at night. That would be just plain foolish.

"I feel so silly," I said, "but I don't even know the way to the boys' side."

"Oh, that's easy," replied Randi. "There's just one path. I'll draw a map for you. All you have to do is follow the path around the lake. There aren't

110

even any turn-offs. Of course it'll be pitch black at night, but you've got a torch, haven't you?"

I nodded.

"Gosh, it's too bad about Ronald Feenie and Harve 'the Knife' Johnson," Randi continued.

"*Who*?" I said. "Are they counsellors on the boys' side?"

Faye and Julie didn't say anything. They looked at Randi.

"Oh, no," Randi replied. "They're the escapees."

"Escapees?" I gasped. "Escapees from where?"

"That lunatic asylum over in Peacham. It's just a small asylum. But these insane murderers got loose a couple of days ago."

"Oh! Oh, right!" said Julie suddenly. "The ones who killed all those—"

"SHHH!" hissed Faye. "Don't say it. There's no point. I'm sure they're not in this area anyway."

Well, I had no idea whether to believe the girls. They probably weren't telling the truth. They were probably making all that stuff up. Then again, I knew they'd sneaked over to Old Meanie's once and watched her television. They'd heard the local news. I hadn't.

Anyway, I didn't think I had much choice. It was either make the night-time trip, or spend the next week-and-a-half knowing that Randi, Faye, and Julie thought I was a complete idiot.

111

Maybe the trip would help build character. The Camp Mohawk brochure promised to do that.

Besides, it *would* be nice to see Logan.

Bed-check is at nine-thirty every night. I don't understand the logic behind it. No one over seven is remotely tired at that hour. So everyone gets up again after bed-check anyway.

On Wednesday night, I wanted to be out of Cabin 7A before bed-check. It would have been easier to wait until afterwards, but I *didn't* want to be wandering around woods infested with murderers at midnight. I wanted to leave as soon as darkness fell. So I tried the *very* oldest trick in history. I stuffed some clothes and things in my sleeping bag to make it look as if I were inside. Then I put a large watermelon (stolen from the kitchen by Randi) at the head end of the sleeping bag and put my pillow over it, as if I were trying to drown out noise.

Everyone except Connie, our counsellor, watched me do this. They all knew what was going on. (Connie was at a counsellors' meeting over at Mrs Means's.) The girls watched me put on a teepee sweater, load my torch with new batteries, and put the map and that daft love-bunny note in my pocket.

Randi walked me to the path around the lake. "If you run into Ronald or Harve the Knife, just fall down and play dead," she advised me. "They'll probably lose interest and leave you alone."

Great, just great.

Randi left me, and I set off down the path, the beam from my torch bouncing ahead of me. I prayed that the batteries in the torch were in good working order and hadn't been sitting in the hardware shop for five years before I bought them.

Crunch, crunch, crunch. I kept stepping on twigs and leaves as I walked along. *Swoosh, swoosh, swoosh.* The water from Lake Duckanawooda lapped at the shore nearby. I wished my trip could be quieter. But it only seemed to get noisier. An owl hooted. Crickets chirped.

I shivered.

I don't know how long I'd been walking when I heard a voice say softly, "There she is." It was a man's voice.

There was a pause. Then another voice said, "That's not her."

"Yes, it is. It must be. I see a light."

I couldn't help it. I forgot what Randi had said about playing dead. Instead I began to scream.

"Go away! Get out! Don't kill me! I've got a kitten at home. He needs me. I've got a gun too."

"Mary Anne?"

Aarghh! How did the escaped murderers know my name?

Then I heard another voice. This time it was a

woman's. "Mary Anne. We know you're there. Stay where you are, okay?"

The voice sounded familiar but . . . maybe there was a third mental-asylum escapee, someone the police didn't know about with a name like Bonnie "the Hatchet" Jones or Goldie "Fast-Finger" Swordman.

"Mary Anne!" the voice called again. "It's me, Connie."

Connie!

"Connie!" I finally replied. "I'm here!" I wasn't lost, but I have to admit I was relieved to be found, even if I was going to be in trouble.

I stood where I was, torch on, and was soon surrounded by Connie, Mrs Means, and two boys who were probably counsellors at Logan's camp. (They were wearing teepee sweatshirts.)

Mrs Means frowned and looked disappointed, but Connie hugged me. "I was so worried about you!" she cried.

"How did you know I was gone—and where to look for me?" I asked.

"Tara told Mrs Means during bed-check that you hadn't been feeling well. When we looked in on you we found the watermelon. Then the story just came out. Tara couldn't help herself."

Connie didn't look too pleased with Tara, which delighted me.

Then Mrs Means said that I would have to be punished. This was my punishment: no swimming

116

for three days. What a tragedy.

One of the boy counsellors made me hand over my note to Logan. "We'll see that he gets it," he said. His voice was sort of strained. Was he making a threat or a promise? I couldn't tell. And I nearly panicked. That note! That wasn't the kind of thing I'd *ever* send to Logan. What would he think when he read it? That I'd gone crazy? That I was more serious about our relationship than he thought? Oh, no. Oh, no. It was too horrible to think about.

Mrs Means spoke to the boys. Then they walked off down the path. Connie, Old Meanie, and I turned around and walked back the way I had come. Nobody said a word the whole way. I was dying to ask whether there really were some escaped lunatics, but I didn't think this was the right time for it. Also, I was beginning to wonder what to expect from Randi, Faye, and Julie when we reached the cabin. On the one hand, I hadn't made it to Logan. On the other hand, it hadn't been my fault. The Terror, one of our own campers, had ruined the adventure (thank goodness).

Mrs Means left us when we got to her cabin. Before she went inside, she gave me a *look* and warned me never to try something like that again, young lady. (Now I see how she got her nickname.) Under ordinary circumstances, I might have cried then, since I was in trouble and I'm not used to being in trouble, but as soon as Old Meanie had disappeared, Connie put her arm around me again.

"I tried to sneak around the lake once," she told me.

"You did?"

"Mm-hmm. To see a boy. When I was a CIT."

I smiled into the darkness.

Back at 7A, we found a few lights on and everyone awake. Connie went next door to talk to the 7B counsellor, and Faye and Julie tiptoed over and joined Randi and me in a huddle on Randi's bunk. The campers watched us solemnly from their own bunks, even Tara, which I thought was odd. Why wasn't she gloating?

For a few seconds the other CITs just stared at me.

"Okay, so I didn't make it," I said crossly.

Faye and Julie continued to stare, mouths slightly open, but Randi whispered, "How far did you get?"

"How far around the lake? I don't know. About halfway, I suppose," I replied.

"*Halfway*? You know, only two other girl CITs have ever tried to sneak around the lake," said Randi. "In the whole history of Camp Mohawk."

So that's why Tara wasn't gloating. She was as awed as Randi. So were the other campers. So were Faye and Julie. I couldn't believe it.

I grinned and shrugged my shoulders. "No-

118

thing to it," I said. "If Tara hadn't tattled," (here was my chance to give Tara a *look* of my own), "I'd have made it all the way around."

Tara actually seemed slightly ashamed.

I knew I wouldn't have to worry about impressing the CITs any more, no matter how I dressed.

"You know what was odd, though?" I went on. "The counsellors from the boys' side took my note and said they'd give it to Logan for me. They said it right in front of Old Meanie. I was surprised. I thought Old Meanie would have torn it up or something. As punishment. Not let it get to Logan."

"Hmm," said Randi, "I wonder what that means."

I wondered, too. And I didn't find out for a while.

FRIDAY

DEAR MUM AND DAD,

Hi. HOW ARE YOU? I'M FINE. CAMP MOHAWK
IS FINE, TOO. MOST OF THE TIME. I MEAN,
YOU KNOW — POISON IVY, CAMP FOOD,
STUPID RULES. BUT I LEARNED HOW TO
CANOE AND I SWAM TO THE MIDDLE OF
LAKE DEKA-DEKA AND BACK, WHICH
EARNED ME A HIAWATHA BADGE. THAT
MEANS I CAN DO ANY WATER SPORT
ANY TIME I WANT. I MIGHT LEARN
TO WATER-SKI.

LOVE LOGAN

MR. AND MRS. LYMAN BRUNO

689 BURNT HILL ROAD

STONEYBROOK, CT 06800

12th CHAPTER

LOGAN

Stacey said I have to write some entries for her daft book, and post them to her in New York when camp's over. I have never kept a diary or a notebook, except for one week after I read *The Diary of Anne Frank*, and that was for English homework. But Stacey wants Camp Mohawk reports for her book from every club member who was there this summer, and that includes me. Okay, here I go.

First of all, I want to say that I wrote my parents a postcard today, making it sound as though water sports are the biggest thing in my life right now. What a lie. Getting my Hiawatha badge *was* exciting, but the postcard doesn't begin to tell the story of what's going on over here on the boys' side of camp.

I was put in Cabin 7A. (The cabin names here

are *so* thought-provoking.) And guess who three of my campers are—Jackie Rodowsky, Buddy Barrett, and Matt Braddock. Matt was put in my cabin because the counsellor and I know enough sign language to be able to communicate with him. And Buddy knows quite a lot of sign language, too, because he's Matt's friend.

Matt and Buddy are fine as campers. . . . Then there's Jackie. I'm exhausted after babysitting for him for just an hour. Imagine sharing a cabin with him for two weeks. The weirdest things have happened. Bunks have collapsed. (No one was hurt.) The door is permanently stuck three inches open. (Mosquitoes, mosquitoes, mosquitoes.) And dried toothpaste is all over the floor. I think Jackie dropped his tube and then stepped on it.

Our other campers are Curtis, who's teaching the kids to play poker; Russell, who spends his days writing poetry to a camper in 8B over on the girls' side; and Thomas, who likes to be called simply T. On the whole, the campers are a good crowd, except for when Jackie goes on a disaster spree. It's the CITs (not including me) that I really worry about. They act as though they've just been let out of prison. Well, we *have* all just been let out of school. But even so.

They are hard to keep up with.

The other CIT in my cabin is Rick. He's crazy. Mr Meanie, the camp director over here (husband of Old Meanie), lets him get away with wearing a

123

flowered Hawaiian shirt over his teepee shirt. Henry and Cliff, the CITs next door in 7B, are never without sunglasses, and spend most of their time working on their tans, spying on the Meanies when Old Meanie comes to visit, and trying to work out how to swap films and get a dirty one for Film Night.

It's important to know all this before I describe what happened at lunch today. I was sitting at Table 7 (whoa, thought-provoking) with the twelve campers, our two counsellors, and we four CITs. We CITs were crowded together at one end of the table discussing whether we thought the Meanies ever watched anything besides old Doris Day films on Mr Meanie's TV, when another counsellor (Meanie's personal assistant, I think) handed me a note.

"From your girlfriend across the lake," he said, and walked away.

My girlfriend? This must have been some kind of joke. One of Rick's, maybe. Or else, maybe Mary Anne really had sent me a note. Either way, I was in for it. I knew that straight away.

Sure enough, Cliff made a grab for the paper, but I pulled it away, I'm pretty quick. I read the note quickly.

So did Cliff. He was reading it over my shoulder, only I didn't know that until it was too late.

124

" 'Love-bunny'?!" hooted Cliff. And then, " '*After*shave'?"

"What about aftershave?" said Rick.

"Who's that from?" asked Henry. "Wait. Is that from the girl who tried to sneak over here with a note last night and didn't make it? I heard about that. She left a watermelon under her pillow to make it look as though she was there at bed-check. A *watermelon*. . . . That girl was coming to see *you*, Logan?"

"I suppose so," I said.

"Boy, I never thought I'd see the actual note," Henry went on.

"Allow me to read it to you," said Cliff, taking it from me because I let him. (The story was out. I was beaten.) "I believe you will find it highly entertaining." Cliff snapped the paper in front of him and cleared his throat. Everyone at our table tuned in for the reading.

Cliff did a pretty good job. In a high, squeaky voice, he read every word from "Dear Logan, I miss you so much!" to "Your love-bunny, Mary Anne XXOO."

I had never been so embarrassed in my life. I had also never been so touched. I guessed that the Meanies had made sure I got the note at lunchtime so that everyone would see it, and that this was some sort of punishment for Mary Anne or me or both of us. But this was the first note I'd ever had from Mary Anne that didn't just say, "Happy birthday", or "Meet me at my locker after class".

Does she really mean those things? I was wondering. Does she really want a yellow—

At that point I realized that absolutely everyone at my table was laughing. They were laughing so hard that Henry and Cliff steamed up their sunglasses and had to take them off. And Jackie Rodowsky choked, knocked over his milk, and then fell out of his chair.

I took a long look at Cliff. Then, very slowly, I loaded my spoon with peas and topped them with creamed sweetcorn. I aimed the spoon at him.

"No way!" said Cliff, pushing his chair back.

I boinged the spoon in his direction anyway. The peas and sweetcorn got him on the forehead. It was a good thing he'd taken his sunglasses off.

Cliff ripped a muffin in half, buttered it, and threw it at me. It missed and hit a kid at the table behind me. Quick as a flash, the kid sucked Coke into his straw and sprayed it over at us. Someone else thought that was a pretty good idea and tried it at his table.

Pandemonium.

Food was flying everywhere. Stuff landed on the ceiling and dripped gooily onto our heads. Milk and Coke shot across the hall in arcs. (Jackie Rodowsky sat on a peanut butter sandwich, but that might have been an accident.) Mr Meanie stood up to yell at us and a glob of pickle splattered on to the teepee on his shirt. When he blew his whistle, mustard squirted out.

By that afternoon, I was in trouble, which shouldn't surprise anyone. Mr Meanie's punishment? I was banned from arts and crafts for three days. What a tragedy.

Rick, Henry, and Cliff looked at me with a little more respect. And my counsellor confessed that he had once started a food fight, too.

Now—I'd better put this notebook of mine away before someone catches me keeping a diary. That would ruin any respect I earned today.

Sunday

Dear Mum,

Guess what -- our cabin is going on an overnight camping trip! I can't wait. Remember when I did that at Camp La Brea in California? Charlene (she's our counsellor) and Amy (the other CIT) and I will be in charge. We have a group of six eleven-year-olds, so it shouldn't be too difficult. The campers are really excited, too. We're busy packing and planning and trying to think of all our scariest ghost stories.

See you in less than a week!

Love,
Dawn

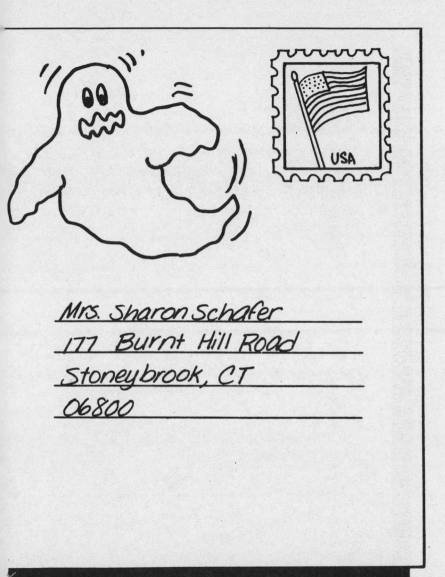

Mrs. Sharon Schafer
177 Burnt Hill Road
Stoneybrook, CT
06800

13th CHAPTER

Dawn

The eleven-year-old campers are the only ones allowed to go on an overnight trip. We go one night, 11B goes the next night. The trip will be great. The food won't be too healthy, but I can't wait for a night under the stars and all that tramping through the woods and nature stuff.

The last week has been great, especially the past couple of days, as our campers become more and more excited about their adventure. They've written and rewritten lists of things to bring. They've also started packing their rucksacks, but they always put things in them that they'll need before they leave, and then they have to unpack. I've seen them put in everything from underwear to an electric toothbrush. (Freddie put the toothbrush in; Heather pointed out its uselessness.)

Speaking of Heather, she hasn't changed a bit.

The other campers think she's weird, so she wasn't too popular when she corrected Freddie's mistake. I just don't understand Heather. She's always pleasant when she says anything. But she speaks so rarely. She reads and writes and sometimes goes to arts and crafts or the nature cabin or quiet places like that. She never goes to the lake for Open Swim, and once she missed her compulsory swimming lesson. I found her in her bunk reading *The Grey King*, by Susan Cooper. She knew she'd missed her lesson, and didn't care. But she wasn't rude about it. The best word I can think of to describe Heather is *inscrutable*, which was on one of my vocabulary lists this year.

The first few days of camp, the other children tried to be nice to Heather, but she wouldn't or couldn't come out of her shell. She never stopped reading and writing and not joining in. Now the girls either tease her or ignore her. I think their feelings are hurt, especially Rachel's. Rachel tries so hard to be friendly to everyone, and she doesn't understand when someone isn't friendly back.

Here is a typical evening in my cabin after bed-check (when the lights are supposed to be off). Slowly torches come on. Charlene draws the curtain around her bed and pretends not to notice the torches. Shari burps loudly and everyone laughs. (Shari can burp on command.) Everyone laughs, that is, except Heather. She has propped her torch on a book and is writing furiously in her diary.

Shari directs another—louder—burp in Heather's direction. I don't think Heather even hears it because she's concentrating so hard, but Donna, from below Shari, says, "Never mind. She's ignoring us again. The best thing to do is give her nothing to ignore. Ignore her back."

"What a baby," says Freddie.

"What a bore," says Caryn.

"That's enough," Charlene finally calls from behind her curtain.

The campers are quiet for about two minutes. Then Rachel leans over the side of her bunk and says, "Psst! Heather! Hey, Heather!"

"Hmm?" replies Heather distractedly.

Rachel drops her voice so Charlene won't hear her. "Want to sneak over to Old Meanie's with us and watch TV?"

Heather finally looks up. She smiles. Rachel smiles back. "No," replies Heather, "but thanks. Really. I just want to stay here."

"Why are you even talking to her?" Caryn asks Rachel.

Rachel shrugs. Heather goes back to her diary. The girls decide not to go to Old Meanie's. And none of them speaks to Heather until the next morning.

Very typical. I feel sorry for Heather, but she doesn't seem to want to change. The girls gave her

133

openings and opportunities, and she ignored them. So now the girls ignore Heather.

At the moment, it is Sunday night, the night before we leave for the big camping trip. And earlier, something awful happened. It was seven o'clock. We had just come back to our cabin after supper, which was disgusting, and were getting ready to have a marathon Monopoly game with 11B, since the weather was drizzly. Otherwise, we would have had to go to Mohawk's outdoor amphitheatre for an astronomy talk by the nature counsellor. After that, we would have watched for falling stars. Frankly, every camper was glad it was raining.

We had just got together the Monopoly set and a supply of popcorn and crisps and were heading for 11B, when the door to 11A opened and Mrs Means strode in. We stopped in our tracks, even though we weren't doing anything wrong. Rachel dropped a bowl of popcorn.

We were surprised that Mrs Means ignored that, but she did. "Charlene," she said, "I need to talk to you."

I knew we were all thinking, Ooh, Charlene's in trouble, but we liked her too much to have said anything.

"Let's go to your sleeping area," said Mrs Means quietly. She took Charlene by the arm, led her to the bed, and drew the curtain around them. Amy and the campers and I didn't budge. We just stared at each other. We knew we should leave Charlene and Mrs Means alone, or at least clean up the popcorn, but we couldn't move. This sounded really serious.

From behind the curtain we could hear the low murmur of voices. Then we heard Charlene begin to cry. A few minutes later, Mrs Means moved the curtain aside and stepped out, leaving Charlene by herself.

"Girls?" she said. (We gathered around her.) "I'm afraid there's been some bad news. Charlene's mother is very ill and Charlene has to go home straight away. Her older brother will be picking her up in a couple of hours."

"Oh, no!" I couldn't help crying out. I made a move towards the curtain.

But Mrs Means stopped me. "Not yet," she said. "Give her some time to herself. Later you can help her pack her things."

"Okay," I replied, drawing back.

"But what about a counsellor for our cabin?" asked Donna, and we all knew that what she was really asking was, "Will we still be able to go on our overnight trip tomorrow?"

"Don't worry," Mrs Means replied. "I've got a list of people who are available as replacement counsellors this summer. Most of them were former CITs here, so they're familiar with the camp. I promise that you'll have a new counsellor tomorrow and that all your activities will go ahead as planned. Meanwhile, Dawn, you're in charge after Charlene leaves." Mrs Means looked at Amy. "That's just because Dawn has had more camping experience than you have. No other reason. You'll be her right-hand CIT."

Amy nodded. Nobody felt like arguing about anything. We were all too stunned by the changes and surprises (even if we did feel relieved about our overnight trip), and we felt too sorry for Charlene.

Mrs Means went next door then to talk to the 11B counsellor. The campers and Amy and I cleared up the popcorn silently. Caryn took the Monopoly board over to 11B and left it there. When she came back, we put away the evening's junk food and lay around on our bunks, reading and doing other Heather-type things.

Charlene left two hours later. We all hugged her goodbye and cried, even Heather.

"Goodbye, Charlene!" we called, as her brother's car drove off. "We hope your mum gets better! Really soon!"

"We'll miss you!" I added.

We filed back into 11A, damp from the rain and as gloomy as Winnie-the-Pooh's friend Eeyore. I had to do something. This could not go on.

"Attention!" I cried, and the campers looked at me, startled. "I'm in charge here, and I have some orders for the rest of the evening." (Freddie and Donna groaned.) "You *must* stay up past midnight!" I announced. (A few smiles appeared.) "You *must* get all that junk food out and *eat it*!" (A giggle.) "Most important, I order you to scare each other to death with ghost stories!"

Everyone began to laugh. They rushed for the junk food. Then they gathered on a couple of the bunks. I think the girls were relieved to know that it was okay to have fun even though Charlene was going through a bad time.

I glanced at Amy and we smiled at each other.

Then I glanced at Heather's bunk and saw her there, curled up with *The Grey King*, looking solitary.

I sighed.

Monday

Dear Henry and Grace,
   Hi, you two! How is New York? I miss you and it a lot. Have you had any other baby-sitters while I've been gone? I can't wait to come back and take you to the new Central Park Zoo, or maybe to the Last Wound-Up to look at toys one afternoon while your parents are working.
   Camp is fine.

Love,
Stacey

Henry and Grace Walker
14 West 81st Street, Apt. 18E
New York, NY 10000

14th CHAPTER

Stacey

Camp is not fine at all. I'm in the infirmary. That's *the infirmary*. Why did Dawn have to show *The Parent Trap* to everyone so many times? (Actually, I'm exaggerating a little. Things aren't bad here.)

How did I end up in the infirmary? Good question. Well, I was just fine when I got to Camp Mohawk last week. And it isn't my diabetes that's the problem, thank goodness. That's entirely under control. This all started a couple of days ago when I began noticing funny things. First of all, I simply didn't feel well. Kind of achy and tired. I thought maybe I really *was* just tired, that I wasn't used to all this exercise and running after six-year-olds twenty-four hours a day. Then I started itching. No matter what I was doing, I would find a new itchy spot somewhere on my body.

I was taking Karen Brewer and Nonie to the washrooms one day when I glanced in the mirror and found a scaly, itchy spot near my mouth.

"What'sh that?" asked Nonie.

"The plague," I replied. I was not in a good mood. I had already found a large red itchy bump on my shoulder that day.

The next day I was helping Monique to make a bracelet in arts and crafts, when she looked at me with alarm. "What's that?" she asked.

I was about to reply, "The plague," again, since I was tired of the question, when I looked where she was pointing. Spreading down my arm, away from the red bump on my shoulder, was a rash. I scratched it experimentally. It was the itchiest of all my itchy things.

Suddenly, I felt chilled. Not the kind of chill you feel when you're sick (that was *one* symptom I didn't have), but the kind of chill you get when you realize something horrible. I was remembering Mrs Mean's announcements on the first night of camp. I was remembering what she'd said about Lyme disease. Flu-like symptoms (I was achy and tired, wasn't I?) and the spreading rash. Well, that bump on my shoulder had spread pretty far.

"Can I go back to the cabin?" I asked the arts and crafts counsellor. "I don't feel very well."

"Of course. Go ahead, Stacey," she replied, worried. "Nonie, go with her. See that she's okay."

Nonie. Of all campers. But I was much too weak to argue.

Nonie led me back to 6B. She stayed ten metres away from me and wouldn't touch me. "I'm sure you're 'tagioush," she said sweetly. "Have you had the chicken pocksh? That thing by your mouth looksh like the chicken pocksh."

Well, I *had* had the chicken pocksh, I mean pox, but I'd heard it was possible to get the disease twice.

The chicken pox? I had Lyme disease *and* the chicken pox?

"And your eyesh look awfully red," Nonie added helpfully as she watched me lie down on my bunk.

Well, maybe red eyes was one of the flu-like symptoms of Lyme disease. More likely, I had developed allergies, possibly to my clothes and sleeping bag.

"Shtashey?" Nonie spoke up tentatively.

"You can go back to arts and crafts now," I told her. "I'll be all right." (I was practically dead.)

"But your rash. It'sh short of all over. Look at your armsh and legsh."

I looked. The rash *was* all over and I itched all over.

I sneezed. Bother allergies! And I realized my stomach didn't feel too good. Probably indigestion.

"You know what, Nonie?" I said, struggling to my feet. "I think I'd better go to the infirmary."

"Do you want me to go with you?" Nonie asked, backing away.

"No, that's okay."

"Oh, thanksh." Nonie rushed out of the cabin. She was probably heading for the washrooms so that she could have a shower and wash off any of my germs that might have hopped on to her.

I walked to the infirmary, feeling extremely sorry for myself. I stepped inside.

The nurse took one look at me and nearly fainted. I must have been sicker than I thought. Leprosy, maybe.

Just in case, I turned around. Nope, no one was behind me. It really was me the nurse was fainting over.

"I have Lyme disease," I told her dispiritedly, as if I barely cared any more. "And allergies and indigestion and the chicken pocksh. I mean, pox."

The nurse recovered. "You don't look too good, that's for sure. Come on and lie down. I'm Miss Dinsmoore. And you're lucky because the camp doctor visits today. He'll be able to prescribe a course of treatment. For now we'd better put something on that poison ivy."

"Poison ivy?" I repeated.

"It's all over you."

"This rash? On my arms and legs?"

"Yes. It's the worst case I've seen in years. What did you do? Roll around in the leaves? You do know what poison ivy looks like, don't you?"

I didn't, but I remembered the nice patch of leaves I'd found to sit in on that first night at camp. And come to think of it, I'd been itchy ever since then. It was just that the rash had been spreading and thickening lately.

I'll spare you the really gruesome details of the doctor's visit, and just tell you that my "Lyme disease" was actually a big mosquito bite surrounded by poison ivy, my red eyes were conjunctivitis (thanks *so* much, Valerie), my sneezing and aches and tiredness were a cold, the disgusting thing by my mouth was impetigo, and all the itchiness was from more insect bites and, of course, the poison ivy. (The indigestion was a nervous stomach, which cleared up as soon as I found out I didn't have Lyme disease.)

"Well," said Miss Dinsmoore, after the doctor had left, "I know you're a really uncomfortable young lady."

I nodded miserably. Maybe they would send me home.

"So you'll be staying here for a few days."

"Here? In the infirmary?"

Miss Dinsmoore nodded. "You'll need a few things."

Karen Brewer was given the job of bringing over my nightgown, toothbrush, injection kit, and the Stephen King book I was now reading.

You might think this was the low point of my Camp Mohawk stay. It wasn't. Getting ill and

145

going to the infirmary was the worst part. Now was the beginning of the best part. First of all, I got a roommate. I'd been the only patient in the infirmary until Miko Tyrrell arrived. Miko was a CIT with a broken leg and a plaster cast up to her thigh. She had been to the casualty department at the hospital in the nearest town. (She broke her leg when she fell off a horse.)

I could see that Miko was in much worse shape than I was, but even so she kept smiling and laughing. And she had lots of visitors. So did I, thanks to my friends and my campers. Soon the infirmary was like a party. Twice, Miss Dinsmoore had to ask us to calm down, although I don't know why, since no one was sleeping. (But Miss Dinsmoore kept taking aspirins.)

Now it's Monday and I'm going to be allowed to leave the infimary soon. My conjunctivitis and impetigo are nearly gone. My cold has cleared up. And although I'm still covered with calamine lotion, my bites and poison ivy feel a *lot* better.

"I wish you could leave soon, too," I said to Miko.

Miko smiled. "Well, at least I get my crutches tomorrow. And I *am* at camp for the rest of the summer. Things could be worse."

She was right. They could be. I knew it the instant Nonie walked in. Now that I wasn't contagious, she wasn't afraid to come near me. Practical-joke worries poured into my head. I

146

remembered peppery chewing gum and a few other things.

But Nonie just sat on the edge of my bed and chatted to Miko and me.

"I'll be helping you back to our cabin tomorrow," she informed me. "I'll carry your things for you."

"Great," I replied, smiling. Maybe camp was okay after all.

Nonie left then. But as she stepped outside and passed the window by my bed, she shot a rubber band in at me. Then she ran away, giggling.

Guess what? I laughed, too.

monday

Dear Bart,
   Well, here I am at camp. It isn't exactly what I expected, but it's, well, an adventure. I guess that's what camp should be, right? How are the Bashers doing? Are you getting them together for team practices, or are your kids all off at camp, too? My kids are getting plenty of softball practice right here (some of them are, anyway), so I'm not too worried about them. In fact, my Krushers challenge your Bashers to a game when we're back in Stoneybrook. And how about if you and I hire a video? I'll watch anything except _Meatballs_!
               – Kristy,
                 Krushers' coach

Bart Taylor

65 Edgerstoune Drive

Stoneybrook, CT 06800

15th CHAPTER

Kristy

Two things my stepfather is always saying (and there are a lot of things Watson is always saying) are: one, that life is full of ups and downs, and two, that you have to take the good with the bad. Since camp is part of life, I suppose it follows the camp would be full of ups and downs, and also that you'd have to take the good with the bad here.

That does seem to be true. Take Charlotte Johanssen. She's an up and a down just by herself. And so are my days here. Some are ups. Some are downs. They all have goods and bads.

After that first awful night here, when Charlotte cried and cried and phoned home, and after letting us know all the things about camp that she's afraid of (horses, the lake, etc.) she's still here. Something is keeping her. (I wish I could

151

talk to Stacey about her, but I don't want to worry Stacey while she's in the infirmary. She's got enough on her mind without having to think about Charlotte.)

One day Charlotte cried because she didn't want to be in a volleyball game against another cabin. (The ball scared her.) Another time she cried because a counsellor shouted at a child. (This had nothing to do with Charlotte.) A third time, she cried during a nature film when a close-up shot of a bullfrog puffing out his throat frightened her.

Each time, I took Char somewhere private and quiet, knelt to her level, took her hands, and said, "You know you can go home, don't you? Becca and I would be so happy if you stayed here, but if you want to go home, you really, really can. It wouldn't be the first time a camper went home early."

And each time, Charlotte sniffled, wiped her eyes, and said she wanted to stay.

"Are you sure?" I asked.

"Positive."

Charlotte did like arts and crafts. And she did like the nature cabin (except for the bullfrog film), and she had very much enjoyed a treasure hunt. She was also nervous but excited about the dance that Mallory and Jessi were teaching my campers. But were those things worth all the tears and fears in between? I wasn't sure. There must have been something else keeping Charlotte at Camp Mohawk. (But I didn't know what it was, and wouldn't find out until later.)

Me? Well, here's a list of the good things I took with the bad:

—sailing
—water-skiing
—swimming
—softball
—watching my children rehearse for Parents' Day

Here's a list of the bad things I took with the good:

—arts and crafts
—the nature cabin
—living with so many people breathing down my neck
—constantly being mentally made up by the other CITs
—being talked into going to that dance on Wednesday (I had worked out a way to skip it.)
—*actually* being made up by the CITs before the dance (This hasn't happened yet.)

I suppose I'd better explain some of these

153

things, since they probably don't make a lot of sense. I think the top list is self-explanatory, except for the last thing. I love sports, so of course I'm in seventh heaven at Camp Mohawk. I even got my Hiawatha badge. But the Parents' Day show . . . my children are having a great time rehearsing their dance routine!

I can't believe it. Even Charlotte, with her homesickness and stage fright, seems to be enjoying herself more. This is for several reasons. For one thing, she's found out that she won't have to perform alone—she's in on a special project with Becca and her other fellow campers. Also, Jessi and Mallory are giving the girls tons of encouragement and attention. I'm sure the campers think they'll go right from Camp Mohawk to the stage at Lincoln Center in New York City. And Jessi and Mal have worked out a sort of dance-and-joke routine (a musical, I suppose) that is fun, funny, and touching.

But the girls' rehearsals are a riot. At first they insisted on wearing tight socks on their feet so that they looked as though they were dancing in ballet shoes. But the socks on the wooden floor were so slippery that everyone kept falling down and Jessi finally had to get mats for the girls to dance on.

Even with the mats, there are falls. Once, Becca (I'm sorry, but she doesn't have much of Jessi's talent) reached a crucial point in the routine. She was supposed to make a leap across the mats to Charlotte and two other girls, who would catch her and slowly lower her face down until she was lying on her stomach. She had done this once before and it was very dramatic-looking. But this time she leaped, arced through the air, and landed on her right foot, which just skidded forward and knocked over Charlotte and a few others.

Everyone burst out laughing. Jessi and Mal called an end to the rehearsal. Even they were laughing.

Meanwhile, some of the bad things that I took with the good were underway. I'm sure I don't have to explain my feelings about arts and crafts and the nature cabin. Those are just not for me. (Or in Watson's words, they're not up my street.) But the rest of it . . . .

It had started on the first day of camp. I could feel the eyes of the other CITs—Tansy, from my cabin, and Lauren and Izzy from 8A—on me at all times. They weren't even subtle about it. They made those outright comments about needing blusher and letting my fringe grow out. In between, they just stared, their eyes calculating. I could see them thinking: pluck her eyebrows, cover up that spot, perhaps get a nose job. Why didn't they just swap me for a new CIT, one with fashion sense?

I began to worry about the CIT dance. I was

definitely not going to it. Not if it meant being scrutinized by Tansy, Izzy, and Lauren. And what if they tried to pair me off with someone?

I could see only one way out.

Poison ivy.

I would roll around in Stacey's leafy patch, and by the night of the dance I'd be a disgusting, itchy mess. I'd be a prisoner in the infirmary.

This was before the CITs' free hour earlier today. As soon as the campers went off with the counsellors, I found myself surrounded by Tansy, Lauren, and Izzy. They sat me in a chair and attacked me—not with fists or words, but with eyebrow pencils, blusher, eye shadow, tweezers, mascara, hair gel, scissors and some things I don't have names for.

They didn't exactly make me up, but they experimented. And all the time they experimented, they shone a bright light in my face, making the torture effect more real. I kept my eyes closed during the ordeal. Finally it was over.

"Open your eyes," said Lauren.

Reluctantly, I did so.

Izzy was holding a mirror in front of me. Some stranger's face was in it.

"Hold it up," I said. "I can't see myself."

Tansy giggled. "That's *you*, Kristy."

I have to admit that I didn't look revolting. I certainly looked better than if I'd been covered with poison ivy. And I certainly felt better than if

156

I'd been covered with poison ivy. But I had a feeling this meant I would have to go to the dance.

"This isn't everyday makeup, is it?" I asked hopefully.

"*No*," said Izzy, smiling. "It's dance makeup and you know it."

I nodded.

"You're going to have a terrific time at the dance," said Tansy.

Maybe, maybe not. Easy for them to say.

The face in the mirror was attractive, pretty, even glamorous. But it wasn't the face of Kristin Amanda Thomas. It was the face of someone who should feel much older, and I didn't feel older. I didn't feel grown-up. I didn't even feel like a Babysitters Club chairman. If I had to go to the dance as a false Kristy, I would be embarrassed. I would be a flop.

And I didn't like this group arrangement, this cabin full of people, with everyone living my life for me. I needed space. I needed privacy. I needed separateness.

Charlotte did, too.

Why on earth was she still at Camp Mohawk?

Tuesday

Hi, Jamine!

Who are you. Camp is fine. I'm looking for a boyfreind. I know that sonds funny but waht I mean is I'm looking for this ~~post post~~ certin boy I saw and I know he likes me and I like him but we don't no each others names. This is a real ~~dli dli~~ problem. I'll will find him though, dont' you worry and il give you a reprot when I see you.

Love your sister,

Claudia

Janine Kishi

50 Bradford

Stoneybrook, Connec 06800

16th CHAPTER

Claudia

Straight away after lunch on Tuesday, I could tell that something was up with my campers. Nine-year-olds are not particularly good at keeping secrets, and my group was no exception, especially when it came to R-O-M-A-N-C-E. And *especially* when they were playing matchmakers (sort of).

When lunch was over, Meghan and the other counsellors took their break, and it was the job of the CITs to go back to the cabins with their campers for a rest hour, during which everyone is supposed to write letters or postcards home. Now Sally, my co-CIT, and I have noticed some dedicated letter-writers among our campers, particularly Vanessa Pike and Gail, the quiet campers. But that day, even they just dashed off sloppy cards and threw down their pens. The campers kept exchanging glances and stifling giggles.

161

"Okay, what's going on?" I asked from my perch on top of Sally's and my bunk.

Nobody tried to hide a thing. The campers all began talking at once.

"We *found* him!" exclaimed Haley.

"Him? Him who?" I asked.

"Him *who*? Your boy, that's who. The boy of your dreams," said little Jayme.

I nearly fainted. "You—you did? How? You mean you know his name?"

"Don't worry about how we did it," said Leeann. "This summer is the fourth one Jayme and I have spent at Camp Mohawk. We know everything—including how to get in touch with the boys' side."

I didn't ask any questions. I had a feeling I was better off not knowing what they knew.

"Your boy," said Jayme importantly, "is named Will Yamakawa. And he'll definitely be at Film Night tonight."

I couldn't believe it! They'd found my mystery boy. I hadn't been able to see him before Film Night, like I'd wanted, but . . . they knew his name. They knew where and when I could meet him. Furthermore, he was Japanese, like me, which would please my parents a great deal. They've never said so, but I'm sure they want me to carry on our family heritage by marrying a Japanese man and having Japanese children. Not that Will and I had plans for that sort of thing yet (he didn't even know me), but Mum and Dad would certainly be pleased to hear about him. My other crushes—Trevor Sandbourne and Austin Bentley—had not been Japanese, and I always knew that disappointed my parents. Boy, what a way to please them—finding the world's nicest (Japanese) boy.

"Gosh!" I exclaimed. "How can I ever thank you? I can't believe what you did." (I hoped nobody would be in any trouble.)

"You can thank us," Haley replied, looking sly, "by giving us a report on the evening. A *full* report," she added.

"I'll do my best," I told the girls.

The CIT film programme was to start at seven-thirty that night. As soon as dinner (if you could call it that) was over, my campers and Sally and I raced back to our cabin, where I dressed in my best teepee clothes and then went to the wash-rooms and put on makeup and jewellery and tied a ribbon in my hair. I didn't want to go all out, though. The dance was the next night, and with any luck I would see Will again. And I would want to look extra-extra-special then.

"Wish me luck!" I called to Vanessa, Haley, and the others, as Sally and I boarded the Camp Mohawk minibus that would drive us around the lake. As we were looking for seats, I wanted to tell Mary Anne that taking the bus around the lake was a lot easier than taking a midnight hike, but she wasn't on the bus. Neither was Dawn. I had heard a rumour about some kind of camp crisis, but no one else knew much about it or seemed too concerned, so the minibus pulled away. I was surprised that Mary Anne was missing a chance to see Logan, though.

Bump, bump, bump. After the world's most jolting ride (not a great idea following a Camp Mohawk dinner) we arrived at the other side of Lake Demidonkey. The boy CITs were waiting to welcome us.

It was Tuesday evening. Camp would be over in four days. There was not a second to lose. I jumped off the bus, spotted Will in the crowd, elbowed my way over to him, and said, "Hi, I'm Claudia Kishi. I met you last week when you came to tell us about the film and the dance."

Will's face broke into a smile. "Claudia," he said. "So that's your name. I was, um, too nervous to ask. How did you know I wanted to meet you? And how did you find out who I am? John didn't introduce Jeremy and me, did he?"

I shook my head. "My campers did a little research," was all I replied.

Will and I were just standing there grinning at each other. Ah, love at first sight, I thought. At last I *truly* knew the meaning of it.

Will walked me into the recreation hall, where the film was to be shown. "Some of my friends tried to get a dirty film," he told me conspiratorially, "but it didn't work out. We're going to see *Meatballs*, with Bill Murray."

"*Meatballs*?" I squeaked. "They're showing us a *camp* film at *camp*?"

Will nodded and made a face.

We sat in the back, where we could talk and not pay attention.

I suppose we talked a little too much.

"Shh!" said someone.

"SHH!" said someone else a moment later.

"*SHHHHHHH!*" said about eight people not long after that.

"Want to go outside?" asked Will.

I nodded. I was afraid to say anything else. I might have been attacked by the audience.

Will and I tiptoed out of the hall. We sat on the concrete steps outside.

"Is this your first summer at Camp Mohawk?" asked Will.

"Yup. Yours?"

"Nope. Third."

"Where are you from?"

"Ashfield, New York. You?"

"Stoneybrook, Connecticut."

After we got the boring facts straight, we began discussing more serious things. I forget how we got on to the subject, but Will told me that his grandmother had always lived with his family.

"Mine, too!" I exclaimed. "We are *so close*, my grandmother and I. I can tell her anything and know she'll understand. My family calls her Mimi. What do you call your grandmother?"

"Well . . . well, um, we called her Tink. It's a long story. But she died last month. She'd been really sick."

"Oh. I'm sorry." At first I didn't know what else to say. Then I said, "I suppose this is a stupid question, but do you miss her?"

"All the time. It's weird. I go around doing whatever I have to do—helping my campers, eating, sleeping, laughing, brushing my teeth. But it's as though there's a hole inside me and I'm always aware of it and it never fills up."

"Do you cry?" I whispered.

"Sometimes."

Just then, the doors burst open and the CITs poured out of the hall. The film was over. Will and I were almost trampled. But we struggled to our feet and followed the others to a camp fire, where we were going to roast marshmallows (mmm, junk food) before we girls had to go back to the other side of the lake.

Will found a stick for us and put four marshmallows on it. He toasted them until the outsides were almost black and the insides were oozing out. Then he pulled the first two off and gave them to me while he ate the others. We licked our fingers and stared at the fire.

Stacey and Kristy were there, but I didn't see them. I wasn't aware of anything except the crackling fire and the moonlight and Will sitting next to me. After a long time, he reached over and took my hand. A chill went down my back. He didn't let go until the CIT minibus pulled up and I reluctantly had to leave him.

Wednesday

Dear Granny and Grandad,

As my friend Claudia would say, "Oh, my lord!" You absolutely will not believe what happened when my campers and I went out on our overnight trip. Parts of it were the scariest times of my life, parts were fun, parts were exciting. Most of it was unexpected. What happened? I think I'd better wait till I get home to tell you. But really and truly we are all safe and sound. Boy, I bet I've got you curious now. Oh, well, I'll probably see you before you get this postcard.

I love you and miss you,
Dawn

Granny and Grandad Porter
747 Bertrand Drive
Stoneybrook, CT
06800

17th CHAPTER

Dawn

The day after Charlene left, Debra arrived. She was going to be our new counsellor. She had been a CIT at Camp Mohawk last summer. That was it. One year of being a CIT. She's only two years older than I am. But she seemed nice. And she didn't mind that her very first activity was to take Amy, me, and six eleven-year-olds on an overnight camping trip.

"I went last summer," she said. "I remember it well."

We were all packed (we had been for days), so we were ready to go. A rucksack and sleeping bag were strapped to each of us, and we planned to take turns carrying the rest of our equipment and provisions—tents, food, cooking stuff, first aid kit, etc.

We set out right after lunch on Monday.

170

We'd walked all of two steps when Heather said, "You've got the compass, haven't you, Debra?"

Debra's eyes opened wide. "Oops," she said. She ran back to the cabin to fetch it.

"Good thinking," I said gratefully to Heather, and the first twinge of worry darkened my good mood.

"And someone's got the extra tinned food, just in case, haven't they?" said Heather.

"Extra tins?" I repeated. I chased Debra back to the cabin.

At last we were really on our way. Debra took the lead, followed by three campers, then Amy, three more campers, and then me, bringing up the rear. Heather was right in front of me. For some reason, I felt relieved.

We'd had an exciting send-off back at camp, with Mrs Means yelling at us to have fun and be careful (she must know Stacey's mother), but now we were on our own. The woods seemed awfully quiet. I tried to think of them simply as peaceful, though. After all, I am a nature girl and should feel at home in the woods.

The route we were to follow was marked by cairns. Every overnight trip follows the same route to the same campsite in the woods. The campsite is about ten kilometres from the centre of Mohawk—a pretty good hike. There are paths throughout the woods near camp, because the younger campers take nature walks and go on short day hikes and that sort of thing. But since Mohawk is in a fairly remote area of the state, it's possible to walk dozens of kilometres from Old Meanie's and still be in the wilderness. (This was according to Heather, who was speaking up and sounding quite knowledgeable.)

Anyway, the route for the overnight trip is marked by those cairns. Cairns are piles of stones that used to be used as memorials (I think), but can also be used as sort of traffic signs in the woods. They tell you which direction to follow to get where you want to go. Let's say you reach a fork in the path and you find a stack of stones piled on the ground near the fork with one stone set to the right of the stack. That cairn would tell you to turn right. If the stone were set to the left of the stack, you would turn left. If you saw simply a stack of stones, that would mean to go straight ahead. Sometimes we would find a straight-ahead cairn where there was no fork. That was just to let us know we were still on the right track. (I found those cairns pretty reassuring.)

Our campers loved watching for the cairns and following their directions. Rachel's bionic vision allowed her to spot a cairn before anyone else, and then yell out where we were going.

"Let's sing," said Caryn after a while. "Let's sing an old rock 'n' roll song from the fifties. Something with a good beat that we can march to."

172

"I've got a song," announced Shari. " 'Monster Mash'. Do you all know that one?"

We weren't sure.

"Well, I'll start singing it. You'll recognize it after a while, I'm sure. They play it on the radio all the time around Hallowe'en. Okay. Here goes. I think I have the words right. *I was working in my lab late one night, when my eyes beheld an eerie sight. For my monster from his slab began to rise, and suddenly, to my surprise—*"

(And suddenly we remembered the song.)

"*He did the Mash!*" we sang, giggling. "*He did the Monster Mash. The Monster Mash. It was a graveyard smash.*" Some of us weren't too sure of the words at this point and were singing, "*It caught on in a flash,*" when Heather, who *hadn't* been singing, cried out, "Uh-oh!"

Her "Uh-oh!" was loud enough to stop the rest of us in our tracks (and in our song).

"What-oh?" said Freddie.

Heather pointed to a cairn we were about to miss because we were so involved in our song. The cairn was at a fork, but it had fallen down. It was just a pile of stones.

"Which way do we turn?" asked Amy nervously.

"Don't worry. I've got a map of the woods," said Debra, pulling it out. She studied it for a moment. Our marching line fell apart as Amy and the campers and I gathered around Debra and the map. I don't know why I even looked at it. I may

173

be good at maths, but I can't read maps very well. I can barely tell my left from my right, let alone north from south or east from west. The map just looked like a lot of squiggly lines. And where were *we* on the map, anyway?

"Okay," said Debra, folding up the map and sticking it under her belt. "We turn left here."

"I don't think so," said Heather. "I think we turn right." But Debra didn't hear her.

We turned left. We walked and walked and marched and marched and sang and sang. By six o'clock we hadn't seen another cairn, but thanks to Debra and her map, we'd made all sorts of turns and would never be able to trace our steps back to that last broken cairn (as if that would have helped).

Debra came to a standstill and so did the rest of us. "Um," she said, "um, I think we're—we're lost. Don't panic, anybody, but I do think we're lost."

I don't know how everyone else felt, but I was ready to panic when Heather said, "I see a clearing." She pointed ahead of us. "Why don't we just make camp here? We have to stop soon anyway to eat and sleep. We can't go tramping through the woods all night."

Everyone was amazed. Until this trip, no one had heard Heather say much more than two sentences at a time. And since her suggestions were reasonable and we were pretty tired, we did exactly as she said. We walked to the clearing and unloaded our gear. Shari, the clown, made a great show of trying to unfasten her pack and toppling over backward, claiming she was off-balance. "I can't get up!" she cried, like a turned-over tortoise.

We began to make camp. We set up the tents. (One collapsed on Freddie.) We unrolled our sleeping bags. We built a fire—finally. We couldn't get it going until Heather stepped in to help us. We stared at her, surprised and grateful. (Nobody had said a mean thing to her since she'd found our campsite.)

"Okay, dinner," announced Debra. You could tell she was trying to be cheerful but was scared to death.

"Dinner?" said Shari. "Don't you mean chow?"

"Whatever."

"I think," spoke up Donna, and I could tell some great plan was about to come pouring out of her mouth, "that we'd better save our rations," (rations?) "and live off the land for a while. Just in case we aren't rescued soon. I'll go and try to catch a rabbit or something. You know, you can even eat rattlesnake meat. It's considered a real delicacy."

"*You* eat it," said Rachel, at the same time Caryn squeaked, "You're going to catch a

175

rattlesnake?" and Freddie said, "And just who is going to skin the rabbit?"

I don't think I need to tell you that what we ate for dinner was just what we had packed—hot dogs and beans, which we cooked over the fire; water from our canteens; and later, marshmallows. (I skipped the marshmallows but I did manage to choke down a hot dog. It was either that or starve. The hot dog was okay as long as I didn't think about what was in it.)

We sat around the campfire with our marshmallows and told ghost stories. We were more scared than usual, which didn't surprise me, considering we were lost.

And then Rachel, bother her, said, "You know, I heard that some insane murderers escaped from that lunatic asylum in Peacham."

A hush fell over the group around the campfire.

"And since we don't know where we are," Rachel continued, "maybe we're quite near Peacham. Maybe we're near the madhouse. Maybe—"

"Aarghh!" (That was sort of a group scream.)

Everyone gobbled their marshmallows, put out the fire, and dived for the safety of the tents, although the tents couldn't keep out mosquitoes, let alone insane murderers.

No one slept much that night and we were all quite tired the next morning, but surprised to find ourselves alive. Furthermore, we were so scared that we decided to eat a very fast breakfast and then just head back to Camp Mohawk, wherever that was. While Debra studied the map, with Heather looking over her shoulder, the rest of us gobbled down some crunchy bars and then began to break camp. We packed up in record time.

We set off again in the direction Debra was sure would lead us back to Camp Mohawk. We walked for three hours.

"My backpack is killing me," announced Freddie.

Heather showed her how to adjust it.

"I'm starving," said Amy.

"We'd better watch our food supply," said Heather.

I realized that the campers seemed somewhat comforted by Heather, and were definitely glad to have her around. Everyone except Debra was going to her with their problems.

"How do you know all this stuff?" I finally asked Heather.

"One of the books I read last week was a camping and survival manual."

I couldn't help smiling at Heather and she actually grinned back at me. I could tell she was proud of herself—and I was proud of her for being proud of herself!

By five o'clock that afternoon we should have been back at Camp Mohawk. But we were nowhere near it. Or maybe we were, since we didn't know where we were. (Or maybe we'd wandered into the back garden of the lunatic asylum.)

"Hey!" cried Amy. "Isn't that where we spent last night?"

We ran to a nearby clearing. There were the remains of our dampened campfire. There were the holes where we had pitched our tents.

"Now what?" The question came from Debra, who didn't look nearly so sure of herself any more.

"May I please have the map?" asked Heather. Debra handed it over.

"I know where we are," said Heather. "I know where we need to go. I think we should stay here tonight because it's a long walk back to camp. Then would you please let me lead the way home tomorrow?"

"Yes!" cried everyone.

We set out very early the next morning, knowing Mrs Means and the rest of the camp were worried to death. We supposed 11B hadn't even been allowed on their overnight trip and we felt bad about that. But we struggled along, following Heather's directions.

After two hours, we heard voices. Then shouts.

"There they are! There they are!" It was a search party from camp. I saw Stacey and Mary Anne and just about everyone.

178

Our group ran to the search party. Mary Anne and I hugged and cried. "I knew something was wrong last night," she said, "but no one would say what it was. I didn't even go to Film Night. Oh, I'm *so* glad to see you. And guess what? You're back in time for the CIT dance!"

I couldn't help laughing. A minute ago I'd been lost in the woods, and now we were talking about dances.

Our rescuers led us back to camp. When we reached it, Mrs Means gave Heather a Camp Mohawk bravery medal.

We all deserved one, I thought, but Heather deserved it the most.

Wednesday

Dear Mimi,

Guess what happened today,
but please, please don't tell
my father, if you see him.
He would kill me, even
though it wasn't my fault.
The other CITs in my cabin
and the cabin next door
dared me to let them pierce
my ears. Even though we
get along okay now, I'm
tired of them still sometimes
trying to prove that I'm
not really trendy.
So I said they could just
go ahead and do it if it
was so important to them.
Did they do it or not? I'll
show you when I get home!

Love and Hugs,
Mary Anne

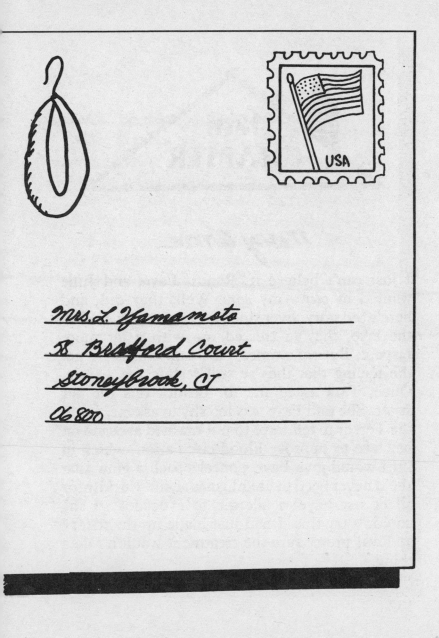

Mrs. L. Yamamoto

58 Bradford Court

Stoneybrook, CT

06800

18th CHAPTER

Mary Anne

I just can't believe it. Randi, Faye, and Julie wanted to *pierce* my *ears*. Well, they did, and here's the story: Ever since I tried to sneak around the lake, they've treated me with a lot more respect. But sometimes—just sometimes—I get the feeling that they're still testing me a little. Once, Tara asked me for beauty tips for her sister. She said Faye was too shy to ask me. I told the Terror to tell Faye to put mashed avocado on her face to improve blood circulation, which in turn would give Faye's cheeks such a glow that she'd never need to use blusher again. Luckily for all of us, Faye is allergic to avocados so she couldn't try this. I had just made up the theory and was pretty sure the treatment wouldn't do a thing.

As the CIT dance approached, the girls started

asking me questions like, Should I wear this blue ribbon in my hair, or this green one? What kind of perfume should I put on to attract a boy without overwhelming him?

I made up answers to the questions. I hoped they were the ones the girls wanted to hear. I hoped they were right.

Then the CITs' Wednesday time-off rolled around. Randi, Faye, Julie, and I were sitting around in 7B when Faye suddenly said, "Hey, Mary Anne, why don't I pierce your ears?"

Well, now, this was an extremely bad idea. For one thing, long ago my father put his foot down— NO PIERCED EARS. A hard and fast rule. For another thing, I'm not even sure I want holes punched through my earlobes.

But Stacey and Claud and Dawn and Jessi and Mal all have pierced ears and they do look pretty terrific. So, with all that in mind, I said, "Well, I don't know."

"You aren't scared, are you?" asked Faye tauntingly.

"No, of course not."

"Then let me pierce them for you."

I sighed. "All right. If it's important to you, go ahead. Pierce my ears."

I knew Dad would kill me, and I was afraid of having a non-professional job (I didn't want to wind up with a raging infection, sharing the infirmary with Miko), but I said yes anyway.

"Yes?" repeated Faye. She looked slightly alarmed.

"Yes," I replied, before I lost my nerve.

"*Yes?*" squeaked Randi and Julie.

"*Yes.*" I was getting impatient.

"Oh. Oh, um, well, let's see what we need here."

There was a long pause. Finally Randi said to Faye, "Come to my bunk. I've got a big needle."

A big needle? Ugh! I thought. But I just smiled at Julie as if to say, "I do mad things like this every day."

Julie attempted to smile back at me.

A moment later, the others returned with a needle. A huge needle.

I gulped. But all I said was, "It has to be really, really sharp."

"You've—you've done this before?" asked Randi.

"Just watched a couple of times," I lied. "You've got the thread, haven't you? And the non-toxic ballpoint pen to mark where you'll make the holes? Oh, and the alcohol?"

I thought that having to track down all those items might put an end to the project, but Faye and Julie went off in search of everything. Randi and I stayed behind. We sat out on the porch, where I pretended to read a book, looking nonchalant, and Randi bit her nails.

I was sure they wouldn't find a non-toxic pen.

184

A moment later, I heard a triumphant voice cry, "We've found everything!"

I dropped my book. "The pen, too?" I asked.

Faye held it out to me. "See? It says 'non-toxic' right here."

"Oh."

We moved back into the cabin. Julie sat me in a chair. Faye shone a light on me. Randi said, "After they're pierced, we'll put some of my earrings in to keep the holes from closing up. We'll sterilize the earring posts first, of course."

"Of course," I said.

"Why—why don't you come and look at my earring box and choose a pair? You need studs with gold posts."

I nodded.

Randi showed me her earring collection. I took much longer than necessary poking through it, and kept purposely holding up earrings that I knew wouldn't be right.

"These?" I asked.

"No, they're hoops," said Randi.

"These?"

"Nope, they've got steel posts."

"Oh. These?"

"Those are okay."

Bother!

"But I was going to wear them to the dance myself," said Randi.

Fantastic!

"Here. Wear these. They're pretty. They're studs. They've got gold posts."

Terrific. Just terrific, I thought. But what I said was, "Gosh, thanks, Randi. I can't wait for Logan to see me in them."

"They ought to go nicely with the yellow flower," replied Randi. "And your yellow ribbon."

"Uh, yeah."

"Well," said Faye, "are—are you ready?"

"Of course." I knew jolly well that neither one of us wanted to go through with this, but *I* wasn't going to be the one to back down.

"Okay, sit here," said Faye, pointing to a chair.

I sat. Julie aimed a light at one of my ears and Randi pulled my hair back.

"You're sure you know what you're doing?" I said to Faye.

"Positive. I just numb your earhole with—Uh-oh. We forgot the ice."

Goodie!

But Julie ran to the hall and was back with a bagful of ice cubes in no time.

"Okay," Faye continued. "I numb your ear. Then I stick the threaded needle through it—I think—then I pull the thread out and put the earring in. Or something like that. I'll just play it by ear."

"By *ear*!" cried Randi, and we began to giggle.

We were still giggling when Faye had finished

numbing my earlobe and was coming at it with the needle. I closed my eyes and gritted my teeth. But I didn't feel a thing. The ice must really have worked.

I opened my eyes. Faye had drawn back. "I can't go through with this," she said. "I just can't. I've never pierced an ear before, and besides, I can't stand the sight of blood."

We began giggling again. We put the instruments of torture away.

I couldn't wait for Faye and Julie and Randi to meet Logan at the dance. Even though I knew we were good friends, I had to prove to them that he was real—and not a twit or a drip.

WEDNESDAY

DEAR KERRY AND HUNTER,
   HI! HOW ARE YOU? HOW ARE YOUR
ALLERGIES, HUNTER? ARE YOU
A-CHOOING EVERYWHERE? I HOPE
YOU'RE BEHAVING FOR MUM
AND DAD. IF YOU'RE NOT, WATCH OUT.
I'LL BE HOME BY THE TIME YOU GET
THIS CARD AND YOU KNOW WHAT I DO
TO LITTLE BROTHERS AND SISTERS WHO
DON'T LIKE TO BE TICKLED!
   TONIGHT THERE'S A DANCE FOR THE
CITs. MARY ANNE WILL BE THERE. SO
WILL MOST OF THE OTHER GIRLS IN THE
BABYSITTERS CLUB. IT'LL BE GREAT.
      BEHAVE YOURSELVES!
         LOVE,
            YOUR BIG BROTHER,
                  LOGAN

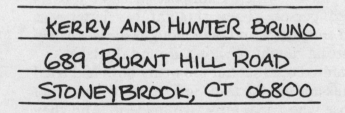

KERRY AND HUNTER BRUNO

689 BURNT HILL ROAD

STONEYBROOK, CT 06800

19th
CHAPTER

LOGAN

Ever since Mary Anne's letter was delivered to me at lunch the other day, all the guys have called her a "feeb", which I suppose means a feeble-minded person. They thought her letter was stupid and gooey, and they thought she was a drip for getting caught sneaking around the lake.

I pointed out that not too many boys had tried to sneak around the lake (so I've heard), and that of those who tried, only two made it. And they were immediately caught on the girls' side by Old Meanie.

Anyway, it was Wednesday night and the recreation hall was ready for the dance. It looked really different from the evening before. The rows of folding chairs from Film Night were gone. The Meanies had hung red and white crêpe paper everywhere and put up bunches of red and

190

white balloons. Hearts were taped to the walls.
Unbelievable—the theme of the dance was
Valentine's Day! Valentine's Day in the middle of
summer! Retch. We didn't know this until we
peeped into the hall after lunch. What a daft idea.
But you could tell the Meanies were really keen.

I wondered, what with Valentine's Day and all,
whether I should try to find a red flower for Mary
Anne, but she had asked for a yellow one, so I
thought I'd better follow instructions. And I
borrowed some aftershave from my counsellor.

Anyway, the afternoon dragged on forever.
Finally supper was over, and the counsellors took
the campers to an astronomy lecture which we
CITs were glad to miss. Instead, we went to our
cabins and got ready for the dance. I put on my
teepee shorts and teepee shirt and tied my teepee
sweater casually around my shoulders. Then I
put on my cleanest teepee socks and my trainers. I
splashed on the aftershave. I was ready.

"That the flower for the feeb?" asked Rick,
pointing to a glass of water next to my bunk. The
glass held a perfectly yellow daisy. Next to it was a
safety pin so I could fasten the flower to Mary
Anne's teepee sweater as soon as she stepped off
the minibus.

"No, it's a flower for Old Meanie," I replied,
punching him on the arm. "I'm trying to impress
her. I want to take her out, then run away to the
Caribbean with her and live there forever. After a

191

year or so, we won't even remember Mr Meanie, although he'll spend the rest of his life hiring private detectives to track us down."

Rick laughed. "Just checking," he said.

"Camp bus is here!" shouted Henry from next door. "Let's go!"

Rick, Henry, Cliff, and I raced out of our cabins and reached the flagpole in the middle of camp, just as the bus pulled to a halt. We gathered around it eagerly. I hadn't seen Mary Anne since the first day of camp. (I was really disappointed last night when Kristy had got off the bus and said there was some emergency or something and Mary Anne wouldn't be able to come to Film Night. The CITs were pretty disappointed, too, and used the word "feeb" a lot more than usual.)

I even began to worry that Mary Anne might not come *tonight*, and then how would I explain things? After that I began to worry that she *would* come. I remembered the first school dance we ever went to together. She was really nervous, but I got her relaxed, and when she was finally relaxed enough to dance, her shoe flew off and sailed across the gym, nearly killing someone.

Oh, brother!

But the second I saw Mary Anne step off the bus, I knew everything was going to be okay. I saw Stacey get off, too (covered with calamine lotion), and Dawn and Claudia, and finally

Kristy, but the only person I greeted was Mary Anne. This was because Mary Anne jumped down the steps of the bus, ran to me, and threw her arms around my neck. As soon as she pulled away, I pinned the flower to her sweater. She beamed.

"You got the note," she whispered. "You remembered. I hope you weren't offended, though. I didn't really mean you to see that note. It was part of something else."

"I guessed as much," I whispered back. "But I didn't mind—much—and I thought you'd like a flower anyway. And look, I put on aftershave."

"You smell nice," said Mary Anne, and we hugged again. When we turned around, we realized we had an audience, a smiling one. I didn't know it until later, but the girl CITs, except for the ones in the Babysitters Club, were smiling because they now saw for themselves that I was a real guy, not a bad one at that, and Mary Anne's real boyfriend.

The boy CITs were just grinning to see that so far Mary Anne wasn't a feeb.

The doors to the hall were standing open and at either side was one of the Meanies. They ushered us inside. As soon as Mary Anne and I were there, the music began, and everyone started to dance. Mary Anne looked at me and said, "I'm getting nervous."

Oh, no. Feeb-dom, here we come, I thought.

But all I said was, "Well, at least your trainer can't fly off."

Mary Anne laughed.

"Want to dance?" I asked her.

She nodded.

The first dance was a fast one, which made Mary Anne even more nervous. Slow ones are better because you don't have to dance so much, just sway around. But it was a fast one, and to make things worse, I could feel everyone watching us. I knew why the boys were watching us. They wanted to see the feeb in action. I suppose the girls wanted to see me in action.

We must have passed their tests, though, because after several more dances, Cliff cut in on us. So I cut in on the couple nearest me, and I swear, for the first few seconds of the dance, I didn't even realize I was dancing with Kristy. She looked really different—terrific. Makeup or some other girl thing, I guess. Anyway, wow!

The dance ended and I looked around for Mary Anne, but I couldn't see her, so I switched partners with Henry. As we were switching, he said, "Nice going, Bruno." I knew he was referring to Mary Anne. And the girl I was dancing with, whose name was Randi, believe it or not, said, smiling, "We've heard a lot about you, Logan."

After the next dance, I *still* couldn't find Mary Anne, but I did spot Claudia dancing with this

194

CIT whose name is Will. I cut in on them, but Claudia seemed a little vague. Very, actually. So vague that I had to get Will back for her. And at *that* point I finally caught sight of Mary Anne dancing with Rick. I whisked her away and wouldn't let anyone cut in on us for the next three dances.

"I'm getting rather tired, Logan," Mary Anne said, as the music stopped.

"Let's sit down, then," I said.

A few card tables had been set up near the table with punch and cubes and things on it. We got some plates of food and sat down. Soon Rick, Henry, Cliff, Stacey, Kristy, Dawn, and some other CITs had joined us.

We talked and laughed and made Meanie jokes.

"Where's Claudia?" Stacey asked at one point, but no one had seen her or Will for a while.

"Nice flower," said Randi to Mary Anne, and she giggled.

"Nice aftershave," said Cliff to me. More laughter.

Not one single person at the tables hadn't heard the story of Mary Anne and the note, but she and her CIT friends told it again anyway, just for fun.

Near the end of the evening, Mary Anne and I crept to a corner of the hall, where I gave her a quick kiss. "See you Saturday," I whispered.

"See you Saturday," she replied.

One more kiss.

195

Thursday

Dear Ashley,

Oh my lord I. have met the boy of my draems. Hes name is Will isnt' that a funny name. But he is realy is the boy of my draems. There was a dance last nigth and we just danced and dased. Then we talked. And Ill will probly never see him agian. Boy is this good matrial for my art you alway say artists need to have expreinces. Well Ive' had plenty of good ones here. I think maybe my heart is breaking so I will be abel to make a good sclupture or painting from my pain.

See you soon,
Claudia

Ashly Wyeth

12 Reilly Ln

Stoneybrook CT 06800

20th CHAPTER

Claudia

I can't believe it's Thursday. I can't believe the dance is over. I can't believe we go home in two days. I can't believe I might never see Will again. Maybe we'll all have to come back here next summer.

But the dance, oh, the dance. Do I sound like someone in a romantic novel? I wouldn't be surprised, because I feel like someone in a romantic novel. I never felt this way about Trevor Sandbourne or Austin Bentley. I might have *said* I felt romantic about Trevor, but it was nothing like this.

Let me backtrack a little to last evening, after supper. I don't know who was more excited about the CIT dance—me or my campers. After all, they had sort of got Will and me together and they knew how I felt about him after Film

Night, so by yesterday, they were just beside themselves.

They all wanted to help me get ready for the dance.

"Wear this hair ribbon!" said Vanessa, bouncing up and down on top of a bunk.

Before I could tell her to stop jumping or she'd either break the bed or hit her head, Haley piped up, "No, wear your hairclips. The ones that look like roses."

"No, no, no, put your hair up!" cried Jayme.

"No, leave it loose," said Leeann. "Boys like it much better that way."

"How would you know?" asked Jayme. "Your hair's only five centimetres long. And you haven't got a boyfriend."

"I've got a *sister*. An *older* one," said Leeann.

"Okay, okay, girls," interrupted Sally, and I looked gratefully at my co-CIT. "Let Claudia arrange her own hair."

"Let me put my makeup on first," I said, heading for the washrooms. "*Then* I'll decide what to do with my hair."

The campers followed me out of the cabin and into the washrooms like a line of ducklings. But they didn't say a word while I did myself up. They just pronounced me fantastic when I had finished.

"Thank you," I said, and once again it was time to board the minibus and go around the lake to the boys' side of camp.

This time, every member of the Babysitters Club, except for our junior members, was on the bus, and we sat together, since we had hardly seen each other since camp began.

No one could get over how fantastic Kristy looked, how tanned Dawn was, how pale Mary Anne still was, how poison ivy-covered Stacey was, or how love-struck I was. I couldn't help it. Will was all I could think of. And when the bus stopped and the door opened I was one of the first girls off.

He was waiting for me.

I ran directly into his arms. Then we linked elbows and headed into the recreation hall.

It was decorated for . . . "Valentine's Day!" I exclaimed.

"Yeah. Weird, huh?" said Will.

"But kind of nice," I conceded.

"I suppose so."

"Romantic."

"Yeahhh. . . . Definitely!"

As soon as the music started, Will and I began to dance. Usually, boys want to eat first (eat a *lot*), then dance a little, then rush back to the food, and so forth. But not Will. We danced and danced and danced. I loved the feel of his arms around me, and mine around him.

Soon people began cutting in on each other and switching partners. The first to do that to us was Logan, because someone had cut in on him and Mary Anne. I don't know why, but after maybe half a minute, Logan left me, found Will, and brought him back. I don't remember much about dancing with Logan, but I remember every second of dancing with Will.

Sometimes we danced slowly, talking softly to each other. Sometimes we danced fast and had to yell at each other over the noise of the crowd. Of course, we saved the personal stuff for the slow dances and the funny stuff for the fast ones. Once when we were dancing fast, and the room was *really* noisy, Will yelled, "Mr Meanie's flies are undone!" They weren't, but it was thrilling to think that you could yell something like that in front of someone without them knowing it.

Then, in a quiet moment, Will whispered into my ear, "You know what? I feel as though Tink is watching me now, and she's happy because she knows I'm happy."

Will's breath on my hair tickled my neck, but all I said was, "That's nice. I hope she's happy for other reasons, too. Do you think that, wherever she is, she's with your grandfather?"

Will looked very serious for a few moments. At last he said, "I don't believe in heaven and hell, but I do believe that the spirits of Tink and Big Papa are together somewhere. So I *know* they're happy. Both of them."

Even though I hadn't known Tink or Big Papa at all, I found that thought comforting.

I was just telling Will that when I felt a tap on

202

my shoulder. I turned around. There was Kristy, smiling bravely. "May I cut in?" she asked.

Oh, my lord. That's something you don't do, no matter what . . . I don't think. Do you cut in on two people in the middle of a slow dance who look as though they're having a conversation? And do you cut in if you're a girl? I wasn't sure, but I let Kristy have Will for a while.

Later, we got some food, then stood at the table and talked to our CIT friends for a few minutes. When the music for another slow dance came on, Will looked at me, stood up, and held out his hand. I put my cup of punch down and let him lead me to the dance floor. We swayed from side to side, and I rested my head on Will's shoulder.

Neither of us spoke a word until Will said, "Let's go outside."

So, just like last night, we slipped through the doors. (The Meanies had abandoned their sentry posts.) Then we sat on the steps, held hands, and talked.

I liked the way Will laced his fingers through mine, but I felt sad. "You know, I'll probably never see you again," I said. "Not here at camp after tonight. And you live in Ashfield and I live in Stoneybrook. We're not exactly next door to each other."

"There's always next summer—" Will began.

"Next summer! What about next month, next *week*?"

Will shrugged. He looked awfully serious.

"I don't want us to end," I said, "but I think we're going to. Even if we are back at camp next summer, a lot can happen in a year."

"I know."

"Maybe we'd better just say goodbye," I said. And the moment I said that, everyone began leaving the hall, and the driver of the minibus turned on the engine and headlights. "Oh!" I cried. "I didn't mean right now! I didn't mean we'd have to say goodbye now. . . ."

"I think we do though," said Will in a choked voice.

I began to cry, too. Tears trickled down my cheeks.

We stood up and Will wrapped his arms around me. "I wish I could hold you forever," he said.

"I wish time could stop right now," I added.

And those were the last words we said to each other. We didn't whisper goodbye. We didn't shout out our addresses or phone numbers. Will opened his arms to let me go, and I climbed the bus steps, the last CIT to board. I sat in the back seat with Stacey and she put her arm around my shoulders, but didn't say anything. I think she knew I wanted to be quiet.

By the time Sally and I reached our cabin, I had stopped crying. We tiptoed inside since the lights were off, and crept to our bunks, but suddenly we were invaded by nine-year-old voices: "How was the dance?"; "Did he kiss you, Claudia?"; "Did he like you with your hair down?"; (That was Leeann, of course.) "What does it feel like when a boy kisses you?"; "Jayme, you can't ask her that!"

I was laughing. So was Sally. Thank goodness for our campers. I told them about the evening. (Well, I left out a few parts.) I even told them about not exchanging addresses. They seemed to understand.

We talked and talked, and finally we fell asleep. The next thing I knew, it was Friday morning.

Thursday

Dear Shannon,

Hi! How's Camp Eerie? (I don't think I'd want to be at your camp on Halloween, if camps were open then.) I've been doing tons of sports. Water-skiing is the best. Maybe I'll try skydiving next. Just kidding. That's one thing you can't do here.

If you had seen me last night, I bet you wouldn't have recognized me. The CIT in my cabin and the ones next door forced me to get dressed up and made up. I didn't look like me at all. I looked like a Kristy Thomas doll. I wonder what Bart would have thought.

Love,
Kristy

Shannon Kilbourne

Camp Eerie

Princeton, MI 48800

21st CHAPTER

Kristy

Well, the dance was last night.

I survived.

It must have been a miracle. I think some dance god was watching over me. I don't love dances, but I've gone to some at school. I've even had fun at a few of them. But here at Camp Mohawk— No, let me rephrase that. Here at Cabins 8A and 8B I have felt so inferior to the other CITs that the last thing I wanted to do was go to a dance with them. Even after our dry-run beauty treatment, I didn't want to go.

But I went.

I suppose I shouldn't say I was *forced* into going, since Tansy, Lauren, and Izzy didn't actually tie me up and carry me onto the minibus and then into the hall on the boys' side of camp; but they might have done that if I had really put my foot down after the makeup session.

Yes, the makeup session.

It went the same way the dry-run had, except for two things. One, we had an audience for part of it. Two, Tansy lent me a pair of her shoes and some of her accessories as well. It's pretty difficult to have the *wrong* clothes at a place where everyone wears the *same* clothes, but as you know, I had those shoes with the Velcro straps. And . . . *no accessories*. No jewellery except for this bracelet I had to weave in arts and crafts, no earrings, hairbands, hair ribbons. Nothing.

So right before dinner, Tansy, Izzy, and Lauren plopped me into a chair and made up my face while our campers were at Open Swim. (Well, Charlotte was just watching Open Swim.)

"But I'm not going to the dance," I said.

"Yes, you are," replied Izzy.

"No, I'm not." (Lauren put something called foundation all over my face.)

"Yes, you are." (Izzy put mascara on my eyelashes.)

"No." (Tansy put on blusher. Then she handed me some blemish remover and told me to cover up the spot on my chin. She wouldn't touch it herself, and I don't blame her. But why did *I* cover it up?)

When my face was made up, I looked in the mirror again. Was that really me? Well, of course it was. And I looked pretty. But I still thought the person in the mirror was some remote film star.

Anyway, after dinner, we CITs had only a half an hour or so before the minibus would take us to the boys' side of Lake Dekadoo. As Tansy, Lauren, Izzy, and I made our final preparations (for take-off?) we drew an audience. Our campers watched us with great interest. They watched as my co-CITs swiftly and expertly put on the proper trainers and accessories. Then they watched as the CITs sat me in a chair and decorated me like a Christmas tree.

"But I'm not going to the dance," I said.

"Yes, you are," replied Lauren. (She put hairslides in my hair.)

"No, I'm not."

"Yes, you are," said Becca Ramsey. "Tansy, let her try your trainers on."

"I'm not going," I repeated.

"No, she isn't," said Charlotte Johanssen. "She's staying here with me." There were tears in Char's eyes and a quaver in her voice.

"Yes. She. Is." That was Izzy. She was putting clip-on earrings on my ears, taking off my stupid bracelet, and lending me a gold one and a necklace.

"Now go into the washrooms and look at yourself," said Lauren.

All of us CITs and campers trooped into the washrooms, where I stood in front of the mirror. I was penned in, hemmed in. I had no space. I

210

couldn't remember the last time I'd been in a washroom alone.

"Don't you think you look beautiful?" asked Tansy.

"Yes."

The minibus pulled up.

"How do you feel?"

"As though I'm going to throw up."

"Good. Stay here with me," said Charlotte.

Becca elbowed Charlotte in the ribs.

"Onto the bus, Kristy," said Izzy, and before I knew it, I was sitting by a window with Mary Anne next to me. Outside, Charlotte was crying loudly.

The bus filled up and pulled away. I did notice that before the campers were out of earshot, Charlotte had stopped crying. I guessed she would be okay until I got back.

Bump, bump, bump. The bus bounced over to the boys' camp. I let everyone get off before me. I watched Mary Anne run into the arms of Logan, and Claudia run into the arms of Will. I considered not getting off the bus, but the driver made me.

Dum, da-dum, dum.

I walked—alone—into a heart-decorated funeral parlour. Well, maybe it wasn't *that* bad.

The first thing that happened was that Tansy appeared at my side and whispered, "When in doubt, hang around the food table. Eating makes you look involved, and when you look involved, you don't stand out so much." She led me through the crowd and over to that table with the punch and cakes and biscuits. I realized I was starving, since I'd been too nervous to eat supper, and anyway, who could have eaten vegetable burgers? How could someone even think them up? I bet the Meanies and the cooks didn't eat them.

Tansy and I each took a cup of punch and a cake. We stood by the table eating until a boy asked Tansy to dance. Then I stood and ate alone until I began to feel sick of cakes. So I approached the dance floor. Lo and behold, a boy asked me to dance! Then Logan cut in on me!! I couldn't believe it!!!

Maybe I was dreaming.

I decided to take the bull by the horns and do something really grown-up. I cut in on Will and Claudia. Will was nice to me, but for some reason, Claudia gave me a dirty look.

Anyway, after a while, everyone was switching partners and I ended up without one, so I went back to the food table, even though the sight of the cakes made me feel sick. Then I noticed that Stacey, Mary Anne, Logan, Dawn, and a group of CITs were sitting around together. Thank goodness. I sat down next to Mary Anne. We talked and laughed. Mary Anne and her co-CITs told the story of Logan and the note. Mary Anne isn't a feeb, but what a thing to do!

I can't say I had a bad time at the CIT dance that night. I also can't say I wasn't glad to see the minibus arrive to take us girls back to our cabins. Immediately, I felt more like myself. I was a Kristy-snake shedding my film star skin so that I could wear my comfortable skin instead. Whew! What a night.

Even though Charlotte had stopped crying by the time I'd left for the dance, I wasn't sure what I'd find when I got back. She survived last night when I went to Film Night, but with Charlotte, you never know.

Tansy and I crept into our cabin. Lights off, everyone asleep, even our counsellor. To be on the safe side, I tiptoed to Charlotte's bunk and leaned down to look at her.

She woke up immediately. "Hi, Kristy," she mumbled.

"Hi, Char. You doing okay?"

"Mm-hmm. How was the dance?"

"Fine, but I'm glad to be back."

"And I'm glad you are back."

"Thanks. Good night, Charlotte."

"Good night, Kristy."

Thursday

Dear Mum and Dad,

I can't believe you phoned the infirmary on Monday. I'm not a baby anymore. Sorry. I know that sounds mean. Actually, I was sort of happy you rang. But . . . I'M NOT A BABY! Anyway, I'm all well, although my skin doesn't look too good. The nurse said I won't have scars or anything, though. I'm really glad you let me stay here at camp. I didn't like camp at first, but it's fun now. Guess what — today is Christmas! Confused? you'll probably know all about it by the time you get this card, because two nights from now I'll be back home with you in the Big Apple.

Your itchy daughter,
Stacey

Mr. and Mrs. Edward McGill

14 West 81st Street, Apt. 12E

New York, NY 10000

22nd CHAPTER

Stacey

I couldn't believe it when my parents phoned me in the infirmary on Monday night. I was all set to go back to my cabin the next day. But the camp had had to keep my parents posted on my progress, and by Monday, Mum and Dad thought I'd been in the infirmary long enough and that maybe they should do something about it. Like take me back to New York and put me in a hospital. In the Poison Ivy Wing, I suppose.

"Mum," I said impatiently over the phone. "All I've got is poison ivy."

"And impetigo and bites and a cold and conjunctivitis. Not to mention diabetes."

"The impetigo, the bites, the cold, and the conjunctivitis are almost gone. And the poison ivy is much better. It's getting to the scabby stage," I added, hoping that if I disgusted my mother she'd change the subject.

"But your diabetes—"

"None of these things is bothering the diabetes. And I'm sticking to my diet and giving myself the injections."

"Well—" Mum began, but before she could finish, Dad got on the extension.

"Hi, darling. Ready to come home?" he asked. "Your mother and I think it's a good idea."

"I don't," I replied.

"Dear?" said Mum.

"Yes?" said both Dad and I.

"I meant your father, darling," Mum told me. "Dear, I don't think she needs to come home after all. Her tests are normal. And she's on the mend."

"My poison ivy is at the scabby stage," I added.

We talked for a few more minutes, and then rang off. The last thing my mother said to me was, "Have fun and be careful."

"So?" said Miko from the next bed as I handed the phone back to Miss Dinsmoore.

"I'm staying," I said, and grinned.

Miko grinned back.

The next day, Miko was allowed to get out of bed and try her crutches. She practised swinging around the room while I packed up my things. I didn't have much to pack and had just about finished when I heard Miko cry, "Whoa-oh! Stacey!"

I spun around in time to see Miko falling. She

had caught the tip of one crutch on a chair leg and was pitching forward. I don't know how I got across the room so fast, but I reached Miko in time to catch her and throw her backwards on to her bed—which I crashed into. Then I fell to the floor.

"Are you okay?" I asked with a gasp, picking myself up.

"I think so. Gosh, Stacey, you saved my life. I could have been killed."

"Oh, no. Please don't say that. I don't want you following me around, doing me favours for the rest of my life."

We both laughed. Then Miko asked, "Are *you* okay?"

A bump was already coming out on my right knee, and another on my right elbow. And I'd scratched myself on a rough spot on the floor. "Three more wounds," I told Miko. "I don't think anyone will notice."

"Honestly, you two are the Accident Twins," pronounced Miss Dinsmoore, who had come running and had overheard the end of our conversation.

"The Accident Twins," I repeated. "I like that."

The nurse checked us over, decided we really were okay, and said I could still return to my cabin that morning. At eleven o'clock, both

218

Nonie and Karen Brewer showed up to escort me back.

"I'll carry your bag for you," Karen said importantly.

"Thank you," I replied. I was fine and could easily have carried the bag myself, since I was about to take over my CIT duties again, but Karen wanted very much to be helpful.

"I'm so glad you're coming back, Stacey!" she said, as she and Nonie skipped ahead of me to Cabin 6B. "You missed some fun, but who knows what might happen next? It could be anything!"

"Are there any other sick people in our cabin now?" I asked warily.

"No. Not unless you count the cut on Monique's finger."

I decided not to. I decided to concentrate on staying well. And I did a good job of it, except for getting a splinter in my hand the second I entered 6B. It was a big splinter and we had to go back to the infirmary so that Miss Dinsmoore could take it out.

But after that I stayed accident-free and germ-free for all of Tuesday night, Wednesday, and Wednesday night. I even got to the boys' side of camp to see the film and attend the CIT dance. And during this time, Nonie didn't play one single joke on me. She didn't so much as aim a rubber band at me.

So you can see why I was suspicious on

Thursday morning when Nonie woke me up early by bouncing on my bed, crying, "Get up, get up, Shtashey! It'sh Chrishmash!"

"Christmas? Oh, Nonie. Stop teasing. Let me sleep. It isn't time to get up yet."

"But it ish! It ish Chrishmash! *Pleash* look out of the window, Shtashey!"

I just knew I was falling for a practical joke, and I hoped that at least I wouldn't get injured. But dragging myself out of bed seemed easier than letting Nonie jump all over me, lisping.

I let Nonie pull me to the window.

Blearily, I looked at the front porch of 6B. I couldn't believe my eyes.

It had snowed! Soft, white powder covered the wooden steps and the swing.

Then I turned around and looked *inside* 6B. How could I have missed what I saw there now? A stuffed stocking hung at the foot of each bunk. A tiny pine tree stood by the doorway. It was decorated with tinsel. A jar of sugar canes stood next to it. A wreath was on the door. And—

"Merry Christmas!" Suddenly the campers, the CITs, and the counsellor from 6A burst into our cabin.

The 6B campers woke up slowly, then became excited and tumbled out of their beds.

"We Christmassed you!" cried a 6A camper.

"Oh, boy!" squealed Monique and Karen and Nonie and the others.

220

I looked questioningly at Barbara, our counsellor.

"During each session of camp," she explained, "one cabin in each age group surprises the other cabin with Christmas in Summer. It's a big secret. No one knows what day will be Christmas."

"Ishn't thish great, Shtashey?" cried Nonie.

"It's merry," I replied.

The 6B campers were tearing into their stockings, while the 6A campers looked on, pleased at what they'd accomplished. Inside the stockings were token gifts—sweets, hairslides, small toys, things the Meanies had provided, I suppose.

"Look in your shtocking, Shtashey," said Nonie.

So I did. Someone had taken great care with it. I found sugarless gum, sugar-free boiled sweets, a pair of teepee earrings, a paperback book—and a box of sticking plasters and a bottle of calamine lotion.

I couldn't help laughing.

Christmas was a wonderful idea. I was liking camp better and better. Too bad I had to go home in two days.

"Nonie," I said, I've got just one question, and I bet you're the 6B camper who can answer it. It's at least seventy degrees now, so what's that snow on our porch?"

Nonie led me to the doorway. We stepped outside. The "snow" rose up in clouds.

"Baby powder," replied Nonie knowingly.

Saturday

Dear Keisha,

Hi, cousin! This is a silly time to be writing you a postcard, because today is the last day of camp. I'll probably post this to you from Stoneybrook when I get home tonight. Anyway, camp has been fun (mostly) but today Mallory and I are nervous. As junior CITs, our job was to teach a dance routine to a group of eight-year-olds for the parents' show today. Boy, has it been a tough job. The girls are not too coordinated. Mal and I want them to do a good job in the show. We also want to prove that we've been responsible, creative junior CITs. Keep your fingers crossed. Love, Jessi

Keisha Ramsey
8320 Wagner Lane
Oakley, NJ 07400

23rd CHAPTER

So camp was nearly over. Mal and I had worked hard and played hard and had a good time—even though the other girls in our cabin hadn't exactly warmed to us, and still called us twins and then laughed, or made jokes about us.

But on this last morning of camp, Mallory and I weren't thinking much about those things. There was far too much to do. Everyone had to be packed up so we would be ready when our parents arrived. We had to clean our cabins. And we had to be prepared for the big Parents' Day show. Every single camper had a part in it—either behind the scenes, like Mal and me, or on stage like our dancers.

"On stage" meant in the amphitheatre. That was the only place big enough to seat the parents. They would sit around and above the performers, who would be on the ground in the middle of the theatre. I supposed that was why a lot of shows had been rained off in other years.

Ours wasn't. The sky was blue and cloudless, the sun shining brightly. I began to worry dreadfully.

"What have we got ourselves into?" I asked Mal in the washrooms that morning. "Our dancers are still clowns. Charlotte hasn't got over her stage fright."

"And we don't know how our cabin-mates, or anyone else, for that matter, are going to react to the musical we wrote," Mal finished for me.

"Right. They might not get the point. They might think we're just trying to make them feel cruel or stupid."

Maybe I'd better stop here and explain the routine Mal and I wrote for our campers. It's a combination dance/play—a mini-musical. It tells a story through both dance and words. And considering what our cabin-mates had put Mal and me through during these last two weeks, the point we were trying to get across wasn't too subtle. It was about friendship and trust and being black or white.

The story is of twin girls who move to a new neighbourhood. Because they're new and are considered "outsiders", most of the other children tease them. They taunt them and jeer at them and insult them. The dancing at that point consists of the taunters surrounding the twins and dancing faster and faster, not allowing them to escape. But one of the neighbourhood children hangs back and just watches. She thinks that what the others are doing is wrong. So she waits until the mean ones have left, and then she introduces herself to the twins. But the twins don't trust her. (Why should they?) However, through some dialogue, some more dance, and some simple acrobatic moves, the audience sees the twins learn to trust, and a friendship begins.

Nice, simple story, huh? Guess who Mal and I cast as the twins?

Becca and Charlotte.

A black girl and a white girl.

The campers in 11B were going to be mortified or angry or both.

"Or maybe ashamed and apologetic," said Mal uncertainly as we left the washrooms for the dining hall and breakfast.

"Oh, boy! I hope so."

Parents' Day is quite an affair. The mums and dads begin arriving around ten. Lunch is at noon, followed by the show, and then . . . camp is over and we leave Teepee Land.

My parents turned up just before ten-thirty. And they brought Squirt with them! I was so happy. I'd been sure they'd leave our baby brother in Connecticut with a sitter. (What sitter? We were all at Camp Mohawk.)

Jessi

Anyway, Squirt cooed and gurgled happily when he saw us. He talked his pretend talk. He hardly knows any words, so when he wants to feel grown-up, he babbles to us. "Moy blur-gum star flit?" he said as soon as Becca and I had covered him with kisses. Then Mama and Daddy and Becca and I hugged and hugged.

Becca and I couldn't wait to show our parents around camp, so when Squirt was settled safely in Daddy's backpack, we set off. Becca and I kept calling out things like, "There's the lake! That's where I water-skied!" (That was me.)

"There's the field!" exclaimed Becca. "Charlotte was playing with an archery set there and thought she shot someone but she hadn't."

You'd think that on Parents' Day, we could have had a decent meal, but old Meanie served those hideous vegetable burgers again. I bet they were left over from Wednesday night. Daddy ate three of them, though. He'll eat anything. Luckily, dessert was ice-cream sundaes.

We were finishing our sundaes when Old Meanie's voice came over the loudspeaker. "Will all campers, CITs, and counsellors please assemble at the amphitheatre now?" she said. "And will all family members please be seated in the theatre by two o'clock?"

"Well," I said to Becca, "this is it. Are you ready?"

She nodded nervously. "Even with my stage

fright. I want to dance well for Mama and Daddy, just like you always do."

"Then let's find Mallory and Char and get going."

The amphitheatre was a madhouse, but the counsellors were good at helping us to get organized quickly. Before Mal and I knew it, it was two o'clock and the show was beginning. The first number was a medley of songs by the campers in 10A and 10B. They sang beautifully, didn't make one mistake, and got lots of applause.

Next the six-year-olds put on a short comedy routine.

Then the nine-year-olds performed a scene from the musical *Annie.*

After that—it was our turn.

The girls playing the children in the neighbourhood were the first on stage. They skipped into the amphitheatre, twirled around once (somebody fell), then linked arms and began a dancing game. At this point Becca and Char, holding hands, walked on stage. The dancing stopped, the play began. When my sister and Charlotte introduced themselves, I noticed a few raised eyebrows in the audience (including my parents), but the play went on. Char was trembling and forgot half her lines. At one point, Becca tripped over her. But the crucial part of the play went fine. To demonstrate that the twins finally trusted their new friend, they had to fall

228

backwards into her arms, not being caught until they'd almost hit the floor. (This is an extremely difficult thing to do, even with your best friend. Try it sometime. Char fell in every rehearsal because she didn't trust her "catcher" enough and would try to stand up at the last second.) But in the play, she was perfect. So was my sister.

Anyway, when our number was over we actually got a standing ovation.

I supposed we'd made our point. But I wasn't sure until later when Mal and I were back in our cabin, packing the last of our things. All of the campers, our CITs, and Autumn, our counsellor, were there, but we were totally silent until Autumn said, "Great play, girls. You two did a terrific job with the younger children."

That broke the ice. I give Mary Oppenheimer a lot of credit for being the first one to say, "Jessi? Mallory? I'm sorry I was mean to you." Because then the other Mary said, "Me, too. Honest." And Mandi said, "If you two like horse stories, try reading *Impossible Charlie*, by Barbara Morgenroth. It's hysterical."

But Maureen didn't say a word. I suppose some people never learn.

It was time to go. Mal and I were packed. Parents and campers were lugging suitcases and boxes and art projects from the cabins to their cars. Mama and Daddy helped with Becca's and my things while I took care of Squirt.

229

The Pikes had driven to camp in two estate cars. (With eight children, they always need those two cars.) And it took them forever to pack up Vanessa, Margo, and Mal, on this side of the lake, and Nicky and the triplets on the other side of the lake. By the way, the reunion of Claire and her sisters was really something. They were excited and on their best behaviour. But—

"This'll never last," Mal whispered to me. "We'll be fighting before we've even left the car-park."

I giggled.

I watched Charlotte climb into a car with her mum and dad. I saw Kristy watching her, too.

"I can't believe she stayed for the two weeks," I said to Kristy, shifting Squirt to my other hip.

"Me neither. But you know what she told me last night? She said, 'I made it, Kristy. I didn't know if I could do it, and I did it.' I think that's what Char's camp experience was about. She wanted to prove to herself that she could stay away from home for two weeks, that she was grown-up enough for that. She didn't do it easily, but she did it."

One after another we were leaving. Dawn and Mary Anne got into a car with Mrs Schafer and Mr Spier, who had driven to Camp Mohawk together. (Dawn and Mary Anne looked smug and happy about this arrangement.)

Kristy and Karen got into an estate car loaded

with people—Kristy's mum and grandmother, Watson, Andrew, and Emily Michelle—before driving around the lake to pick up David Michael.

And Claudia was picked up by her parents. She'd wanted Mimi to come, but Mimi wasn't feeling well and had stayed at home with Janine taking care of her.

Last but not least, just before my family drove off, I saw Stacey climbing into her parents' car so I rolled down my window and yelled to her, "I'll post you the diary on Monday!"

And she shouted back, "Okay. Thanks. . . . Have fun and be careful!"

Everyone in her car laughed.

Camp Mohawk was over.

Dear Stacey,

Hello from beautiful Stoneybrook! I'm glad to be back and not glad to be back. What I mean is, I can't water-ski here, but it really is nice to be home and to see Andrew and Emily and my brothers and everyone. It's especially nice to be myself again!

Big Krushers game against the Bashers coming up. Keep your fingers crossed!

Love, Kristy

Dear Stace,

Hi. I'm glad to be back but im' worryed about Mimi. I dont thinck she feels to good. Wasnt camp fun, thought? I had a good time. You will never guess waht. As a surprize my campers got willis addres for me I dos' no how they got it but Vanessa pike gave it to me after we were all bake in stoneybrooke. Should I writ him a leter?

Love
Claud

P.S. Today is the thrid day in a row Ive' worn somthing with no TP on it.

Dear Stacey,

How is your poison ivy? I am fine. I am back at home. I am glad to be here. I can't believe I hardly ever saw you at camp. Mummy and Daddy are very proud of me for staying there. They said I can go to Camp Mohawk next summer if I want to, but if I don't want to it's all right and I don't have to.

I really, really, really, really miss you.

Love, Charlotte Johanssen

Dear Stacey,
Merry Christmas!
Love, Nonie

EPILOGUE

Stacey

Thanksh, Nonie, I thought.

Gosh, camp really had generated a lot of mail. Since I love mail, this is fine. One piece of mail I got was from Logan. The envelope contained his diary entries. I stuck them into the diary we girls had been passing around on our side of Lake Whatever.

I *love* having the diary. It's the perfect record of our experiences (good and bad) at Camp Mohawk. In fact, it's a really good book, so I decided to write a few pages at the end to wind things up, and to put in some photographs to illustrate it. Most of us had taken cameras with us to camp, and as we got our film developed, we swapped pictures.

This is how I finished the book:

I, Stacey McGill, am recovered, except from my diabetes, of course. My poison ivy has gone. I hope to heaven that I never get poison ivy again. If I go back to Camp Mohawk, I'll know where not to sit. Nonie and I ended up friends and send each other Christmas cards all the time. Merry Chrishmash, Nonie!

I might as well finish Claudia's story with, "Claudia and Will, sitting in a tree, K-I-S-S-I-N-G!" They haven't actually seen each other since the night of the dance, but Claud *did* decide to write to Will, and he wrote back, so she wrote back, then he wrote back, etc. They didn't have to end their relationship after all.

Kristy is glad to be home and sometimes puts on mascara. Then she puts on her baseball cap and goes out to coach the Krushers. The mascara is in case she runs into Bart coaching the Bashers.

Mary Anne ended up being pretty friendly with the other CITs. They write letters sometimes, but Mary Anne says she bets it won't last *too* long. She has also firmly, definitely, positively, certainly, absolutely decided never, ever to have her ears pierced because she cannot forget the sight of that needle coming towards her. She says it appears to her in nightmares, but I think she's teasing.

Dawn, our nature girl, hasn't got over her experience in the woods. It scared her, but she's pleased with herself for having got through it. She's thinking of signing up for Outward Bound next year. That's where they give you all this

235

survival training, then send you out in the wilderness to be on your own for three days, with nothing but a few matches or something like that. Dawn and Heather write long letters to each other. Heather will not be going back to camp.

Mal and Jessi are still best, best friends. They'd already read *Impossible Charlie*, by Barbara Morgenroth, but they read it again, because they knew it had taken Mandi courage to tell them about it. Then they wrote to her, saying they'd enjoyed the story. And Mandi wrote back!

So I suppose all's well that ends well. I know that's a corny way to finish a book, but Mallory is the writer among us, not me, and this is the best I can do.

The End
by Anastasia Elizabeth McGill
(otherwise known as Stacey)